SEVEN STORIES

GW00728906

The *Oxford Progressive English Readers* series provides a wide range of reading for learners of English.

Each book in the series has been written to follow the strict guidelines of a syllabus, wordlist and structure list. The texts are graded according to these guidelines; Grade 1 at a 1,400 word level, Grade 2 at a 2,100 word level, Grade 3 at a 3,100 word level, Grade 4 at a 3,700 word level and Grade 5 at a 5,000 word level.

The latest methods of text analysis, using specially designed software, ensure that readability is carefully controlled at every level. Any new words which are vital to the mood and style of the story are explained within the text, and reoccur throughout for maximum reinforcement. New language items are also clarified by attractive illustrations.

Each book has a short section containing carefully graded exercises and controlled activities, which test both global and specific understanding.

Seven Stories

H.G. Wells

Hong Kong
Oxford University Press
Oxford Singapore Tokyo

Oxford University Press

Oxford   New York   Toronto
Kuala Lumpur   Singapore   Hong Kong   Tokyo
Delhi   Bombay   Calcutta   Madras   Karachi
Nairobi   Dar es Salaam   Cape Town
Melbourne   Auckland   Madrid

and associated companies in
Berlin   Ibadan

Oxford is a trade mark of Oxford University Press

First published 1992
Third impression 1994

Illustrated by Choy Man Yung
Syllabus designer: David Foulds
Text processing and analysis by Luxfield Consultants Ltd.

ISBN 0 19 585470 5

Printed in Hong Kong
Published by Oxford University Press (Hong Kong) Ltd
18/F Warwick House, Taikoo Place, 979 King's Road,
Quarry Bay, Hong Kong

CONTENTS

THE MOTH

Hapley and Pawkins

You have probably heard of Hapley — not W. T. Hapley, the son, but the famous Hapley, Hapley the scientist who studied insects. If you have, you will know of the great quarrel between Hapley and Professor Pawkins. However, you may not know how it ended.

It began many years ago. Pawkins had written a scientific article on microlepidoptera (whatever they might be) and in it he declared that a new type of this insect, discovered by Hapley, was not really a new type at all. It was no different from others that were already known. Hapley, always quick-tempered, produced an angry reply defending his discovery. Pawkins answered it by suggesting that Hapley's ability to study and observe was as imperfect as his microscope. Hapley, when he replied to that, spoke of 'clumsy collectors', 'clumsier methods', and so on. It was war.

From then on, the two great men quarrelled on every possible subject concerning insects, and on every possible occasion. I think that Pawkins was more often right than Hapley, but Hapley was a more skilful speaker. He had a great amount of energy and a great ability to make his enemy look foolish. Pawkins, on the other hand, was a man dull in speech, and dull in appearance. He had a reputation too, for dishonesty, for allowing students who paid to pass examinations. So the young men gave Hapley their support. These battles continued for many years, and the hatred between the two men became deeper.

In 1891 Pawkins, whose health had been bad for some time, wrote a paper about the death's-head moth. This work was far from being his best, and it contained a number of mistakes which Hapley could attack. Hapley must have worked day and night preparing to do so.

He wrote a very long and detailed speech in which he showed his enemy no mercy. Every mistake was pointed out, and Pawkins was made to look a complete fool. One can imagine Hapley's untidy black hair, and strange, dark eyes flashing as he spoke. Pawkins made a reply, but it was hesitating and badly thought out, although full of hatred. Pawkins certainly wished to hurt Hapley, but he did not have the ability to do so. Few of those who heard him, however, — I was absent from that meeting — realized how ill he was.

After this successful attack, Hapley decided to defeat his enemy completely. He wrote an article on the life of moths in general, which was filled with arguments especially written to show that Pawkins's ideas were worthless, and that his life's work had no value. The violence of the language was extraordinary, but the arguments were good ones and must have made Pawkins feel ashamed and confused.

Scientists everywhere now waited for a reply from Pawkins. There was no doubt he would try to give one. He had always had courage. But Pawkins fell ill and died.

Strangely enough, this was perhaps the best reply he could have made, for it weakened Hapley's support. Those who had happily encouraged him in the fight now became serious. They were sure that the disappointment of defeat had helped to kill Pawkins. There must be a limit even to scientific argument, said these serious people. Another fierce attack, written by Hapley some time before, appeared in a science paper on the day before the funeral. I don't think Hapley tried very hard to stop it. So people remembered Hapley's merciless attacks on his enemy, and forgot his enemy's faults. They especially disliked this latest attack on a man who had just died. Even the daily newspapers thought it wrong.

In his private thoughts, Hapley could not forgive
Pawkins for dying. It was, firstly, a selfish trick to escape
from final defeat. And, secondly, it left a strange sense of
emptiness in Hapley's mind. For twenty years he had
worked hard, often until very late at night, seven days a   5
week. All this time he had used his microscope, his
collecting-net, and his pen for one thing only — the
destruction of Pawkins's reputation. And his own
reputation had grown as a result of his efforts.

It was true that their last quarrel had killed Pawkins,   10
but it also troubled and disturbed Hapley. His doctor
advised him to give up work for a time, and rest. So
Hapley went to a quiet village in the country. There he
thought day and night about Pawkins and the things it
was now impossible to say about him.   15

The moth appears

At last, Hapley began to realize what this was doing to
his mind. He determined to fight against it, and to get
Pawkins completely out of his thoughts. He started by
trying to read stories. But every time he picked up a book,   20
he could see Pawkins. White-faced, he was making his
last speech, and every sentence of it contained a mistake
that Hapley was eager to attack.

So Hapley tried playing chess, and found that this
helped him feel calmer. He soon became an expert, and   25
he began to beat everyone he played. But when his
opponent's king began to look like Pawkins, he decided
to give up.

The best kind of rest is a change of work. Hapley
decided to study water plants. He had one of his   30
microscopes and Halibut's book sent down from London.
He thought that if he could start a quarrel with Halibut,
he might be able to forget about Pawkins. And soon he
was hard at work with his usual energy, studying the water
plants growing near the village.   35

It was on his third day with the water plants that he noticed a new addition to the local insect life. He was working late, and the only light in the room came from a little lamp with a green shade. With one eye, he was looking down the microscope. With the other one, he could see the table-cloth. The pattern on the grey cloth was coloured red, gold and pale blue. At one point, it seemed to start moving.

Hapley suddenly lifted his head and looked with both eyes. His mouth fell open with amazement. Part of the pattern was a large moth with its wings spread out.

It was strange it should be in the room, for all the windows were closed. Strange it should not have attracted his attention before when it flew to its present position. Strange it should match the table-cloth. Strangest of all that to him, Hapley, the great expert on moths, it was completely unknown. There was no mistake. It was crawling slowly towards the foot of the lamp.

'A new kind of moth, by heaven! And in England!' said Hapley, staring.

Then he suddenly thought of Pawkins. Nothing could have made Pawkins more envious ... And Pawkins was dead! Something about the head and body of the insect reminded him of Pawkins, just as the chess king had.

'Confound Pawkins!' said Hapley. 'But I must catch this.' And looking round for some means of capturing the moth, he got slowly out of his chair. Suddenly the insect rose, struck the edge of the lampshade — Hapley heard the noise — and disappeared into the shadows.

In a moment Hapley had removed the shade, so that the whole room was lit up. Although the thing had disappeared, his sharp eyes soon found it on the wall near the door. He went towards it, holding the lampshade, reaching up to trap it. Before he reached it, however, it 5 had risen and was flying round the room. Like all moths, it flew with sudden movements and sudden turns, and seemed to disappear and then re-appear again. Once Hapley struck with the lampshade, and missed. Then he struck at it again. 10

The third time he hit his microscope. The instrument fell against the lamp, knocked it over, and fell noisily to the floor. The lamp remained on the table and, very unluckily, went out. Hapley was left in the dark. He jumped nervously when he felt the strange moth hit his 15 face.

It was annoying. He had no light. If he opened the door of the room, the thing would get away. In the darkness he saw Pawkins quite clearly, laughing at him. Pawkins always had an unpleasant laugh. He swore angrily and 20 banged the floor with his foot.

There was a nervous knock at the door.

Then it opened a little, very slowly.

Hapley's landlady

The frightened face of the owner of the house appeared 25 behind a pink candle flame. 'What was that terrible noise?' she said. 'Has anything — ' The strange moth appeared close to the slightly open door.

'Shut that door!' said Hapley, and suddenly rushed at her. 30

The door was shut with a bang. Hapley was left alone in the dark. Then in the silence that followed, he heard the old lady hurry upstairs, lock herself in her room, drag something heavy across the floor and put it against the door. 35

It became clear to Hapley that his behaviour and appearance had been strange and frightening. Confound the moth! And Pawkins! However, it would be a pity to lose the moth now.

5   He felt his way to the cupboard and found the matches, after knocking over a vase, which fell down with a crash. He turned and held up a lighted candle. No moth could be seen. Yet once, for a moment, the thing seemed to be flying round his head. Hapley very suddenly decided to

10 give up and go to bed. But he was excited. All night long he dreamed of the moth, Pawkins, and the grey-haired lady who owned the house. Twice in the night he got up and put his head under the cold water tap.

One thing was very clear to him. The old lady could

15 not possibly understand about the strange moth, especially as he had failed to catch it. No one but a scientist could understand how he felt. She was probably frightened at his behaviour, and yet he did not know how he could explain it.

20   In the morning, he decided to say nothing about the events of the night. After breakfast, he saw the old lady in the garden, and decided to go and talk to her. He would remove any fears she might have about him. He talked to her about vegetables and flowers, bees and honey, and

25 the price of fruit. She replied in her usual manner, but she looked at him a little suspiciously. And as they walked about the garden, she walked in such a way that there was always a row of flowers, or bushes, or plants, or something, between them. After a while, he began to feel

30 extremely annoyed at this and, to hide his annoyance, went indoors. Presently, he came out again to go for a walk.

During the walk, although he did his best not to, he kept thinking of the moth, which reminded him so

35 strangely of Pawkins. Once he saw it quite clearly, with its wings spread out, on the old stone wall that runs along the west side of the park. But when he went up to it, it

was only the natural pattern and colour of the stone. 'Instead of moths trying to look like stones,' he said, 'stones are now trying to look like moths!' Once he thought something flew round his head but, with an effort, he did not pay any attention to it.

In the afternoon Hapley visited the minister. They sat talking in the garden of the church. 'Look at that moth,' said Hapley suddenly, pointing to the end of the wooden bench.

'Where?' said the minister.

'You don't see a moth on the end of the bench?' said Hapley.

'Certainly not,' said the minister.

Hapley was amazed. The minister was staring at him. Clearly the man saw nothing.

That night, Hapley found the moth crawling over his bed. He sat down on the edge of the bed and argued with himself. Was it imaginary? He felt he was going mad. And he fought against the madness with the same silent energy he had once used against Pawkins. In fact habit made him feel that he was still in a struggle with Pawkins. He knew quite a lot about psychology. He knew that when the mind is tired, it imagines things. But not only did he see the moth, he had heard it when it touched the lampshade. And he had felt it strike his face in the dark.

He looked at it. It was not like anything in a dream. It was perfectly clear and solid in the candlelight. He saw the hairy body, the legs, the wings which had even been a little damaged. He suddenly felt angry with himself for being afraid of a little insect.

Hapley behaves strangely

The old lady had asked her servant to sleep with her that night. She was afraid of being alone. She had also locked the door, and put a heavy table against it. They listened and talked in whispers after they had gone to bed, but nothing happened to frighten them. About 11.00 p.m. they had dared to put out the candle, and both had fallen asleep. Suddenly they awoke, and sat up in bed, listening in the darkness.

5   They could hear feet walking up and down in Hapley's room. A chair was knocked over, and there was a violent bang against a wall. Then something made of glass smashed on the floor. Suddenly the door of the room opened, and they heard him on the stairs. They held on 10 to each other tightly, listening. He seemed to be dancing up and down the stairs. He went down three or four steps quickly, then up again, then all the way down to the bottom. Something else fell with a crash, and then they heard the front door-key turn. He was 15 opening the front door.

They hurried to the window. It was a dark, grey night. The moon was almost hidden 20 by cloud. The trees in front of the house were black against the pale road. They saw Hapley, looking 25 like a ghost in his nightshirt, running up and down the road, and beating at the air above his head. Sometimes he 30 would stop. Sometimes he would rush at something they could not see. Sometimes he would creep towards it carefully. At last he disappeared along the road towards the wood. Then, while they argued about who should go down and lock 35 the door, he returned. He was walking very fast, and he came straight into the house, closed the door quietly, and went up to his bedroom. After that everything was quiet.

'Mrs Colville,' said Hapley, calling downstairs next morning, 'I hope I did not frighten you last night?'

Mrs Colville said nothing.

'The fact is, I am a sleep-walker. I walk in my sleep. The last two nights I have been without my sleeping medicine. There is nothing to be frightened of, really. I am sorry I made such a fool of myself. I'll go to the chemist's shop and get something that will make me sleep tonight. I ought to have done that yesterday.'

But on the road to the chemist's, the moth came to Hapley again. The thing flew into his face, and he tried to strike it with his hat to defend himself. Then anger, the old anger he had so often felt against Pawkins, came back to him. He continued on his way, jumping and striking at the dancing insect. Suddenly he stepped on nothing, and fell.

When he managed to sit up, he was in a deep ditch by the side of the road, and his leg was twisted under him. The strange moth was still flying round his head.

He struck at it with his hand and, turning his head, saw two men approaching him. One was the village doctor. Hapley realized this was lucky for him. But he also realized, very clearly, that no one would ever be able to see the strange moth, except himself. So it was better to be silent about it.

Hapley in the asylum

Late that night his broken leg was more comfortable, but he had a slight fever, and he forgot this decision. He was lying flat on his bed, and he began to look around the room to see if the moth was still there. He tried not to do this, but couldn't control his eyes. He soon saw the thing resting close to his hand, by the bed-lamp, on the green table-cloth. The wings moved. With sudden anger, he tried to strike it with his hand, and the nurse woke up with a little scream. He had missed it.

'That moth!' he cried, and then he added, 'It was my imagination. Nothing!'

All the time he could quite clearly see the insect. It flew here and there around the room. And he could quite clearly understand that the nurse could not see it, and looked at him strangely. He must keep control of himself. But as the night passed, his fever grew worse, and the fear of seeing the moth made him see it. He tried to get out of bed to catch it, though his leg was on fire with pain. The nurse had to struggle with him.

Because of this, they tied him down to the bed. When this happened, the moth grew braver, and once he felt it settle on his hair. Then, because he tried to strike it with great force, they tied his arms also. Now the moth came and crawled over his face, and Hapley cried, swore, screamed, prayed for them to take it off him, but all this was of no use.

The doctor was a fool, inexperienced, and knew nothing of the science of psychology. He just said there was no moth. If he had had any intelligence, he might have saved Hapley. He might have pretended the moth was real, and given him something to cover his face. But, as I say, the doctor was a fool, and Hapley was tied to his bed until the leg was healed. And all the time, the imaginary moth was crawling over him. It never left him while he was awake, and it grew into a monster in his dreams. While he was awake, he desired only to sleep, and from his sleep he awoke screaming.

So now Hapley will spend the rest of his life in a mental asylum, worried by a moth that no one else can see. The asylum doctor says it is imaginary. But Hapley, when he is calm and can talk, says it is the ghost of Pawkins, and therefore rare and worth catching.

THE INEXPERIENCED GHOST

Clayton catches a ghost

I can clearly remember the scene in which Clayton told his last story. He sat in the corner by the warm fire, for the greater part of the time. Sanderson sat beside him, smoking his favourite pipe. Evans was there, and Wish, who was a fine actor and a modest man.

We had all come down to the Mermaid Club that Saturday morning, except Clayton, who had slept there during the night. We had all just finished an excellent dinner, and were sitting together afterwards. We made ourselves comfortable, and were prepared to hear Clayton's story.

When Clayton began to speak, we naturally thought he was lying. Perhaps he really was lying — the reader will soon be able to decide that for himself. Certainly he began like a man who is telling a true story. But at that point, we thought he was only acting, in order to make his story more entertaining.

After a long look at the wood burning in the fire, he started, 'You know I was alone here last night?'

'Except for the servants,' said Wish.

'Who sleep at the back of the building,' said Clayton. 'Yes. Well — ' He looked at his cigar for a minute, as if he still dared not tell his secret. Then he said quietly, 'I caught a ghost!'

'You caught a ghost, did you?' said Sanderson. 'Where is it?'

And Evans, who admired Clayton greatly, shouted, 'You caught a ghost did you, Clayton? I'm so glad! Now tell us all about it.'

Clayton said he would in a minute, and asked Evans to shut the door.

He looked at me and explained, 'We don't want to frighten our excellent servants with stories of ghosts in this place. And this, you know, wasn't a regular ghost. I mean, I don't think it will come again — ever.'

'Are you telling us you didn't keep it?' said Sanderson.

'I was too kind to do that,' said Clayton. And Sanderson said he was surprised.

We laughed. Clayton continued, with a slight smile, 'You may laugh. But in fact it really was a ghost. I know that I saw it, as clearly as I can see you now. I'm not joking. I mean what I say.'

Sanderson smoked his pipe. His red eyes looked at Clayton. He said nothing. 'You know, I never believed in ghosts or anything like that before. And then I caught one for myself.'

'You talked to it?' asked Wish.

'For an hour, probably.'

'Was the conversation interesting?' I said. I was one of those who still thought he was joking.

Clayton did not answer my question. 'The poor thing was in trouble,' he said.

'Crying?' someone asked.

Clayton sighed at the memory. 'Yes, he was,' he said. 'Yes.' And then, 'Poor thing! Yes.'

'Where did you hit it?' asked Evans.

Clayton did not answer Evans either. 'I never realized,' he said, 'what a miserable thing a ghost might be.'

He made us wait for a few minutes, while he searched in his pockets for matches to light his cigar. Then he said at last, 'I treated it badly. A person keeps his character even after he has become a ghost. We often forget that. A person who is firm and strong in his character when he is alive will also be so when he is a ghost. This poor creature was neither firm nor strong.' Clayton suddenly looked around the room. 'I say it with all kindness, but that is the plain truth. I knew he had a weak character as soon as I saw him.'

He stopped for a minute to light his cigar.

'I discovered him, you know, at the top of the staircase.
5   His back was towards me, and I saw him first. At once I knew he was a ghost. He was white and I could see through him. I could see the wall through him. He looked as if he didn't know what he wanted to do. One of his hands was on the wall. The other was held over his
10 mouth. Like this.'

'What did he look like?' asked Sanderson.

The weak ghost

'Thin. Like many young men, he had a long, thin neck. And his head was small, with short hair and
15 rather ugly ears. His shoulders were narrow, and he wore a shabby jacket and trousers. That's what he looked like to me. I came very quietly up the staircase.
20 I did not carry a light, you know. But there is a lamp on the table at the bottom of the stairs, and I saw him as I came
25 up. I stood still and looked at him. I wasn't afraid. I think that in most affairs like this one is not as afraid, or excited,
30 as one expects. I was surprised and interested. I thought, "Here's a ghost at last. And I haven't believed in ghosts for a single moment in the last twenty-five years."'

Wish looked serious. He did not seem to be enjoying
35 Clayton's performance.

'He realized I was there almost immediately. He turned his head, and I saw the face of a young man with a small, pointed nose and a weak-looking chin. For an instant, we stood watching one another. Then he seemed to remember what he was. He turned round and stuck out his face. Then, raising his arms and spreading his hands out just like a proper ghost, he came towards me. As he did so, his mouth opened, and a very faint, "Boo" came from him. No it wasn't the least dreadful. I'd had my dinner and a bottle or two of wine, and I was no more frightened than if a frog had attacked me. "Boo," I said. "Nonsense. You don't belong to this place. What are you doing here?"

'He decided to try again. "Boo-oo," he said.

'"Boo-oo!" I said back to him. "Are you a member of this club?" And to show he didn't worry me, I stepped through a corner of him, and began to light a candle. "Are you a member?" I repeated.

'He moved a little away from me. He looked very disappointed. "No," he said, "I'm not a member. I'm a ghost."

'"But that doesn't allow you to be inside the Mermaid Club. Is there anyone you want to see, perhaps?" As steadily as possible, to show him I wasn't afraid, I lit my candle, and turned to him. "What are you doing here?" I said.

'He had put his hands down, and stopped his booing. Now he stood looking confused and awkward, the ghost of a weak, silly young man. "I'm haunting," he said.

'"You haven't any right to," I said in a quiet voice.

'"I'm a ghost," he said, defending himself.

'"Maybe you are, but you haven't any right to haunt here. This is a respectable private club. People often come here with children. You might easily meet a poor little child and give it a terrible fright. I suppose you didn't think of that."

'"No, sir," he said, "I didn't."

'"You should have done. You haven't any claim on this place have you? You weren't murdered here, or anything like that?"

'"No, sir; but I thought that because it was an old
5 building, and — "

'"That's no excuse. Your being here is a mistake," I said in a firm but friendly voice. "If I were you I wouldn't wait for dawn — I'd disappear now."

'He gave me a worried look. "The fact is, sir — " he
10 began.

'"I'd disappear," I repeated, this time quite loudly.

'"The fact is, sir, that — somehow — I can't."

'"You can't?"

'"No, sir. There's something I've forgotten. I've been
15 here since midnight last night. I've been hiding in the cupboards of the empty bedrooms, and places like that. I'm worried. I've never come haunting before, and something is wrong."

'"Something is wrong?"

20 "Yes, sir. I've tried to do it several times, and I've failed. I've forgotten some little thing, and I can't get back."

'That, you know, rather surprised me. He looked so miserable that I spoke to him quite kindly, and said, "That's strange. Come into my room, and tell me more
25 about it." I tried to take him by the arm. But, of course, it was like trying to hold smoke in my hand. I had forgotten my room number, I think. I remember going into several rooms — all fortunately empty — until I saw my luggage. "Here we are," I said, "sit down, and tell me all
30 about it. It seems to me, my friend, that you are in trouble."'

The ghost's unhappy life

'Well, he said he wouldn't sit down. He preferred to float about the room. And he did, and in a little time we were
35 having a long and serious talk. And soon, you know, the

effects of the wine began to leave me. And I began to realize what a strange affair this was. There he was, a real ghost, floating about in this nice, clean, old bedroom. Except for his faint voice, he made no noise. And, through him, you could see the ornaments, and pictures, and furniture. He was telling me about his unhappy little life, that had recently ended on earth. He hadn't a particularly honest face, you know, but I'm sure he told me the truth. He told me how he had been killed. He went into a room with a candle to look for escaping gas. When the accident happened, he was an English master in a London private school.'

'Poor young fellow!' I said.

'That's what I thought, and the more he talked, the more I thought it. There he was, without purpose in life or in death. He said unkind things about his father and mother, and his school teachers, and about everyone who had known him well. He had lacked confidence in himself and had been nervous. He said that nobody had ever respected him or understood him. He had never had a real friend in the world, I think, and he had never had any success. He had been poor at games, and had failed examinations. "Some people are like that," he said. "Whenever I went into the examination room or anywhere, I seemed to forget everything." He intended getting married, to someone like himself, of course, when the accident with the gas ended his life. "And where are you now?" I asked.

'He couldn't explain that clearly. I understood from what he said that he was in a place for souls that had been neither bad nor good. But I don't know. He talked too much about his own troubles to give me a clear idea of the place, or country, where you go after you die — the Other Side of Things, you know. Wherever he was, he seems to have made friends with ghosts like himself — ghosts of weak young men. They talked a lot about "going haunting" and things like that. Yes — going haunting! They seemed to think that haunting was a great adventure, but most of them were afraid to do it. However, he had been persuaded to try.'

'Really?' said Wish. He seemed to be talking to the fire.

5 'That was what he told me,' said Clayton, modestly. 'He floated around, talking in his thin little voice about his miserable existence. He was thinner and sillier than if he had been real and alive. Only then, you know, he would not have been in my bedroom here — if he had been

10 alive. I should have kicked him out.'

'Of course,' said Evans, 'there are poor humans like that.'

'And they have souls like the rest of us,' said I.

'I began to respect him a little when I realized that he

15 knew the kind of person he was. The mess he had made of haunting had made him very unhappy. He had been told it would be fun. He had come expecting it to be fun. And here it was, just another failure for him. He said he had always been a failure, a complete failure. He said,

20 and I can quite believe it, that in his life nothing he tried had been successful. And in death, he was a failure too. If he had had some sympathy perhaps — he paused when he said this and looked at me — things might have been better for him. He went on to say that nobody had ever

25 given him the amount of sympathy I was giving him now.'

The signs

'I could see what he wanted at once, and I was determined to avoid it. Perhaps it was cruel of me, but I did not want to be the man who was his Only Real Friend. I did not want to be the person who received all his complaints

30 and confessions. I got up quietly. "Don't think about these things too much," I said. "You must try to get out of here — get away immediately. You must make an effort. Try."

'"I can't," he said.

'"Just try," I said, and he tried.'

'Tried!' said Sanderson. 'How?'

'Signs,' said Clayton.

'Signs?'

'He made signs with his hands. That's how he had come in, and that's how he had to get out again. Lord! What trouble I had with him!'

'But how could signs — ' I began.

'My dear man,' said Clayton, turning to me, 'you want everything clear. I don't know how. All I know is that he did. After a long time, you know, he managed to make the right signs, and then he was gone.'

'Did you,' said Sanderson slowly, 'observe the signs?'

'Yes,' said Clayton, and thought for a moment. 'It was very strange,' he said. 'There we were, this thin, unhappy ghost and I, in that silent room, in this silent, empty building. Not a sound, except for our voices. There was the single candle burning on the table by the bed, and that was all. And strange things happened. "I can't," he said, "I shall never — !" And suddenly he sat down on a little chair at the foot of the bed, and began to cry. Lord! What an unhappy thing he seemed!

'"Stop it," I said, and tried to give him a comforting squeeze. My hand went right through him! By that time, you know, I wasn't as brave as before. I began to realize how mysterious it all was. I remember pulling back my hand out of him, and saying to him, "Stop crying and try." And to encourage him and help him I began to try also.'

'What!' said Sanderson, 'the signs?'

'Yes, the signs.'

'This is interesting,' said Sanderson. 'You mean that this ghost of yours revealed — '

'Did his best to reveal the way to the Other Side of Things? Yes.'

'He didn't,' said Wish, 'he couldn't. Or you'd have gone there too.'

'That's exactly it,' said Clayton, looking thoughtful.

For just a little while there was silence.

'And at last he did it?' said Sanderson.

'At last he did it. He took a long time, but he did it at last — quite suddenly. He seemed to give up, we had an argument, and he complained he couldn't do it while I looked at him. "I really can't." he said. "I get so nervous when someone looks at me." Of course, I wanted to see, but he refused to let me, and suddenly I felt as tired as a dog — he made me tired. "All right," I said, "I won't look at you," and turned towards the mirror by the bed.

The ghost disappears

'He started very fast. I tried to watch by looking in the mirror. His arms went round, and then his hands, and then with a rush he came to the last sign of all. For this one, you stand straight up, and open out your arms like this. He did this, and then he wasn't there! He wasn't! I turned from the mirror towards him. There was nothing! I was alone in the room. I was amazed. What had happened? Had anything happened? Had I been dreaming? It was a strange feeling. Lord! It was strange!'

Clayton looked at his cigar for a moment. 'That's all that happened,' he said.

'And then you went to bed?' asked Evans.

'What else was there to do?'

I looked at Wish. We wanted to laugh, but the way Clayton looked prevented us.

'And about these signs?' said Sanderson.

'I believe I could do them now.'

'Oh!' said Sanderson, and took out his tobacco. 'Why don't you do them now?' he said, beginning to fill his pipe.

'That's what I'm going to do,' said Clayton.

'They won't work,' said Evans.

'If they do — ' I suggested.

'You know, I'd prefer you not to,' said Wish, stretching his legs.

'Why?' asked Evans.

'I'd prefer him not to,' said Wish.

'But he doesn't know them properly,' said Sanderson, putting too much tobacco into his pipe.

'It doesn't matter. I'd prefer him not to,' said Wish.

We argued with Wish. He said that if Clayton made those signs, he would be making fun of something serious.

'But you don't believe — ?' I said. Wish glanced at Clayton, who was now staring into the fire.

'I do — more than half, I do,' said Wish.

'Clayton,' said I, 'you're a good liar. Most of the story was all right. But that disappearance ... Tell us you made up the whole thing.'

He paid no attention, but stood up and faced me. For a moment he looked at his feet thoughtfully. Then he stared at the opposite wall. He raised his two hands slowly to the level of his eyes, and —

'Don't begin,' said Wish.

'It's all right!' said Evans. 'You don't think nonsense of this sort is going to carry Clayton to the Other Side of Things. It won't. You may try if you want, Clayton, until your arms drop off your body.'

'I don't believe that,' said Wish, and stood up. 'You've made me half believe in that story, and I don't want to see you do this thing.'

'Goodness!' I said, 'Wish is frightened.'

'I am,' said Wish, quite sincerely. 'I believe that if he makes the right signs, he'll go.'

'He won't,' I cried. 'He can't. We all know that there's only one way out of this world for men, and Clayton is thirty years from that. Besides ... And such a ghost! Do you think — '

⁵ Wish interrupted me by moving away. He walked out from among our chairs, and stood beside the table. 'Clayton,' he said, 'you're a fool.'

Clayton, with humour in his eye, smiled back at him. 'Wish,' he said, 'is right and all you others are wrong. I ¹⁰ shall go. I shall get to the end of these signals and, when the last one is made, the floor here will be empty. You will be full of amazement, and a respectable, well-dressed gentleman weighing 210 pounds will drop into the world of ghosts. I'm certain. You will be certain too. I refuse to ¹⁵ argue any more. Let me try this thing.'

'No!' said Wish, and took a step forward and stopped. Clayton had already raised his hands again.

By that time, you know, we were all nervous, mainly because of the behaviour of Wish. We sat watching ²⁰ Clayton. I had a tight, stiff feeling all over my body. Clayton bowed with dignity, and began to wave his hands and arms before us. As he came towards the end, our excitement grew, although we tried to hide it. The last sign was to open his arms wide, and hold up his face. ²⁵ When, at last, he started this, I stopped breathing. It was silly, of course, but you know that ghost-story feeling. It was after dinner, in a strange old house, full of shadows. Would he, after all ..?

There he stood for one long moment. There was no ³⁰ sound in the room. With his arms open and his face turned up, he was bright and solid in the light of the hanging lamp. We watched for the whole of that moment which seemed to last an hour. And then, from all of us, there was a sigh of the greatest relief. He wasn't going. We could ³⁵ see him. It was all nonsense. He had told a clever story and almost made us believe him, that was all! And then, in that moment, Clayton's face changed.

It changed. It changed
as a house with all its lights on
changes when the lights are put out.
His eyes were suddenly eyes that were fixed.
His smile was fixed. He stood there very still.

5

That was a long moment too. And then, you know,
chairs were pushed back, things were falling, and we were
all moving. His knees started to bend, and he fell forwards.
Evans rose and caught him in his arms …

It shocked us all. I suppose that for a minute no one said a thing. We believed it, yet could not believe it. I recovered from my confusion to find that I was kneeling beside him. His vest and shirt were torn open, and Sanderson's hand was on his heart ...

The fact that lay before us was quite a simple one. We did not have to hurry to understand it. It lay there for an hour. And it is still in my memory now. Clayton had indeed gone into the world that lies so near to, and so far from our own. And he had gone there by the only road a human may take. Did he go because he imitated a ghost? Or was he killed by heart failure, as the doctors might say? I do not know. That question will be unsolved until the final solution of all things comes to us. But I do know for certain that, at the exact moment, at the exact instant that he made the final signal, he changed, and fell, and lay before us — dead!

THE NEW ACCELERATOR

Gibberne's preparation

My old friend Professor Gibberne is like the man who, when looking for a penny, finds a pound. I have heard before of scientists who make important discoveries by accident. But there has never been one as important as this. I honestly believe it is going to change the way people live. And it was made while he was looking for a simple medicine, to help people who were a little short of energy. I have taken the stuff several times now, and the best thing I can do is describe the effect it had on me. It will become clear that amazing things can happen to people who search for new experiences.

Professor Gibberne is my neighbour in Folkestone. As everyone knows, he is an expert on substances that affect the brain. In the last few years, he has been busy working on medicines which make people more lively and energetic. And, even before the discovery of the New Accelerator, he had been very successful with them. Science is grateful to him for at least three valuable discoveries, and Gibberne B is especially well known.

'But I am not satisfied with any of these things yet,' he told me nearly a year ago. 'Either they increase the energy of the brain without affecting the body, or they make the body more active, and leave the brain untouched. What I want is something that affects both, something that will make a man three times as lively as anyone else. That's the thing I'm looking for.'

'It would make a man tired,' I said.

'That is very certain. And he'd eat double, or more — and all that. But just think what the thing would mean.

Imagine you had a little bottle like this.' He held up a small green one. 'And imagine that in this precious bottle, there was the power to think twice as fast, move twice as quickly, and do twice as much work as you usually do.'

5   'But is such a thing possible?'

'I believe so. If it isn't, I've wasted my time for a year. Some preparations I've tried seem to have some effect. It would be good enough even if it were only one and a half times as fast.'

10   'It would be,' I said.

'If you were a busy politician, for example, with lots of urgent things to do, and no time to do them in?'

'I could give some to my typist,' I said.

'And have twice as much time. And think if you, for
15   example, wanted to finish a book.'

'Usually,' I said, 'I wish I'd never begun them.'

'Or a doctor with too much work, who wants to sit down and think about one of his patients. Or a lawyer, or a man studying for an examination?'

20   'It would be worth a dollar a drop, and more, to men like that,' I said.

'Or in a fight, where everything depends on your speed,' said Gibberne.

'Or in a game,' I said.

25   'If I can find this thing, it will do you no harm at all, except make your youth just a tiny bit shorter. You will have had twice as much life as anyone else — '

'I wonder,' I said thoughtfully, 'in a game — would it be fair?'

30   'You have to decide that yourself,' said Gibberne.

'And you really think such a thing is possible,' I said.

'As possible,' said Gibberne glancing at something going past the window, 'as a bus. You know — '

He paused and smiled. 'I think I know the stuff …
35   Already I've got some ideas about how to make it.' The nervous smile on his face showed he meant this seriously. He rarely talked of his experiments until they were very

near the end. 'And it may be — I shouldn't be surprised
if — it may even do it at a greater rate than twice.'

'It will be a rather important discovery,' I said.

'It will be, I think, rather important.'

But I don't think that he knew how important, in spite   5
of what he said.

The preparation is finished

I remember that later we had several talks about the stuff.
'The New Accelerator', he called it, and each time he
spoke of it, his voice became more confident. Sometimes   10
he talked nervously of the unexpected results it might
have on the body if it was used. And then he would get
a little unhappy. At other times he thought of the money,
and we spent hours discussing how much it might earn
for him. 'It's a good thing,' said Gibberne, 'an excellent   15
thing. I know we've given the world something. It's only
right that the world should pay. I agree that scientists must
have dignity, but I don't understand why they shouldn't
have money as well.'

My own interest in the Accelerator certainly did not   20
grow less. I have always been interested in problems of
space and time, and Gibberne seemed to be preparing
something to increase the speed of life. If a man drank
such a preparation, he would live an active life indeed.
But he would be an adult at eleven, middle-aged at   25
twenty-five, and an old man at thirty.

In the weeks that followed, Gibberne was much too
busy to see me, but on the 7th or 8th of August, he told
me that his experiment was in its final stage, and on the
10th, that it was completed. The New Accelerator was   30
really in existence. I met him in the centre of Folkestone
— I think I was going to get my hair cut. He came hurrying
to meet me and told me at once of his success. I remember
that his eyes were unusually bright, and his face red with
excitement. And I noticed also how quickly he walked.   35

'It's finished,' he cried, seizing my hand and speaking very fast. 'Come up to my house and see.'

'Really?'

'Really!' he shouted. 'You won't believe it! Come up and see.'

'And it does — twice?'

'It does more, much more. It frightens me. Come up and see the stuff. Taste it! Try it! It's the most amazing stuff on earth!' He held my arm so tightly, and walked so quickly, that I was forced to run. Shouting together, we ran along the street. A whole bus full of people turned and stared at us as they went past. It was one of those hot, clear days you often get in Folkestone. Everything was bright, and although there was some wind, it was not enough to cool me or prevent me from sweating. Short of breath, I asked him to go slower.

'I'm not walking fast, am I?' cried Gibberne, and he slowed down to a quick march.

'You've been drinking some of that stuff,' I said.

'No,' he said, 'only a drop of water from a bottle that had contained the stuff, and which I washed out last night.'

'And it goes twice?' I said. Gratefully, I saw we were approaching his gate.

'It goes a thousand times, many thousand times!' cried Gibberne, pulling me through the gate of his garden.

'Unbelievable!' I said, and followed him to the door.

'I don't know how many times it goes,' he said, with his key in his hand.

'Do you — '

'We'll talk about the stuff later. But now, I want you to try it.'   5

Trying the preparation

'Try the stuff?' I said as he pushed me into his room.

'There it is in that little green bottle. Unless you're afraid.'

I am really a rather careful man, and although I enjoy   10
reading about adventures, I have no desire to take part in them. I felt fear. But on the other hand, I didn't want to show it. I hesitated.

'You say you've tried it?' I said.

'I've tried it,' he said, 'and I don't look hurt by it, do I?   15
And I feel — '

'Give it to me,' I said and sat down. 'How do you drink it?'

'With water,' said Gibberne, putting a jug on his desk.
He stood in front of the desk, looking down at me in the   20
chair. His manner suddenly became like a doctor's. 'It's strange stuff, you know. I must warn you that you must shut your eyes as soon as you've swallowed it. Then open them very carefully in about two minutes. One still sees. But if the eyes are opened too soon, they receive a shock   25
which makes everything spin in confusion. Keep them shut.'

'Shut,' I said. 'Good!'

'And be completely still. Don't move. If you do, you may hit something and have a nasty accident. Remember   30
you will be going several thousand times faster than you ever did before. And your heart, muscles, brain, everything — will be going faster too. You will hit something hard without knowing it. You won't know it. You'll feel just as you do now. Only everything in the   35

world will seem to be going many thousand times more
slowly than it ever went before. That's what makes it so
strange.'

I said, 'Do you mean — '

'You'll see,' said he, and glanced at his desk. 'Glasses,'
he said, 'water. All here. You mustn't take too much for
the first attempt.' The little bottle was emptied of its
precious contents. 'Don't forget what I told you,' he said.
'Sit with your eyes tightly shut and in complete stillness
for two minutes. Then you will hear me speak.'

He added about an inch of water to each glass.

'Remember too, don't put your glass down. Hold it in
your hand and put your hand on your knee. Yes — like
that. And now — '

He lifted his glass.

'The New Accelerator,' I said.

'The New Accelerator,' he answered, and we touched
glasses and drank. Instantly I closed my eyes.

For some time, my mind was completely blank. Then
I heard Gibberne telling me to wake up, and I opened
my eyes. There he stood as he had been standing
before. His glass was still in his
hand. It was empty, that was
the only difference.

'Well?' said I.

'Nothing strange?'

'Nothing. A
slight feeling
of excitement,
perhaps.
Nothing else.'

'Sounds?'

'Things are quiet,' I said. 'Yes! They are quiet. Except for a faint sound like rain drops falling. What is it?'

He said something I didn't understand about sound being slowed down. Then he looked towards the window. 'Have you ever seen a curtain before a window fixed like that before?'

I looked up. There was the end of the curtain high in the air, and unmoving. It looked like a curtain which is being blown by the wind. But, as I said, it did not move.

'No,' I said. 'That is strange.'

'And here,' he said, and opened my hand that held the glass. Naturally, I expected the glass to smash. But it did not even seem to move. It hung there in the air. 'An object falls about sixteen feet in the first second,' said Gibberne. 'This glass is falling sixteen feet a second now. Only it hasn't been falling yet for the hundredth part of a second. That helps you to understand the speed of my New Accelerator.' And he waved his hand round and round, over and under the slowly sinking glass. Finally he took it by the bottom, pulled it down, and placed it very carefully on the table. 'Eh?' he said to me, and laughed.

'That seems all right,' I said, and began very carefully to get up from my chair. I felt perfectly well, very light and comfortable, and quite confident in my mind. I did not feel at all strange. I knew that my heart, for example, was beating a thousand times a second, but it did not make me feel uncomfortable. I looked out of the window.

In the park

A man on a bicycle, his head down, chased after a bus with a cloud of dust behind it. But the man, the machines, and the dust were not moving. I stared in amazement at this sight. 'Gibberne,' I cried, 'how long will this stuff last?'

'I don't know!' he answered. 'Some minutes, I think. But it will seem like hours. After a while, I believe it will wear off quite suddenly.'

I felt proud, as I realized that I did not feel frightened. I suppose it was because there were two of us. 'Should we go out?' I asked.

'Why not?'

'They'll see us.'

'They won't. Certainly not! Why, we shall be going a thousand times faster than usual. Come along! Which way shall we go? Window or door?'

We went out of the window.

I have heard or read of no stranger experience than the one Gibberne and I had in Folkestone that day. We went out by his gate into the road, and carefully studied the unmoving traffic. When we looked closely, we could see that the wheels of the bus were moving, although very slowly. And the conductor's lower jaw. He must have been beginning to say something. But everything else was still. And it was silent except for a faint sound coming from one man's throat! The driver, conductor, and eleven passengers were like statues. They were like ourselves and yet not like ourselves. At the beginning the effect was strange, at the end — unpleasant. A man and a girl laughed at one another, and their faces, attractive at first, seemed after a time, ugly. A woman, who looked out of the window towards Gibberne's house, seemed to have the blank expression of the dead. We looked at them, and we laughed at them. Then we felt a sort of disgust, and turned away and walked towards the park.

'Look here,' Gibberne cried suddenly.

He pointed, and there, its wings moving so slowly that every beat could be seen, was a bee. We went ahead of it into the park.

There everything seemed madder than ever. There was a band playing. But all we heard from it was a kind of quiet sigh. Sometimes this was combined with a noise like the slow tick of a giant clock.

People stood on the grass as if they had been suddenly frozen. Some had one leg in the air. I passed a dog with all four legs off the ground, and watched as it completed its jump and slowly sank to the earth. 'Look! Look here!' cried Gibberne. We stopped for a moment before a splendid person dressed completely in white. He had turned to wink at two smiling young ladies he was passing. A wink, when you are able to study it closely, is not an attractive thing. It loses its quality of joy, and one notices that the eye does not completely close. A line of white can be seen at the lower edge of the eyelid.

'Remind me never to wink again,' I said.

'Or smile,' said Gibberne, looking at the ladies' teeth.

'Somehow it seems very hot,' said I. 'Let's go slower.'

'Oh, come along!' said Gibberne.

We walked between the rows of chairs on the path. Many of the people sitting there seemed quite natural. But there was one purple-faced gentleman. Without appearing to move, he struggled violently in the wind to turn the pages of his newspaper. There were plenty of other signs that made us think a strong wind was blowing, although we could not feel it.

We walked a little way from the crowd, and turned to observe it. It was like looking at a great, wonderful picture. And I considered myself to have an enormous advantage over everyone in it. All that I had thought and done, since drinking the stuff, had happened in less than a second of their time. 'The New Accelerator — ' I began, but Gibberne interrupted me.

The effects wear off

'There's that awful old woman!' he said.

'What old woman?'

'She lives next door to me and has a dog that never stops barking. Oh God! The temptation is too strong.' Sometimes Gibberne's behaviour is very like a child's. Before I could say anything, he had run forward, and seized the unfortunate animal. Then he turned and ran

violently with it towards a
cliff. It was most extraordinary.
The little creature, you know, didn't
bark or struggle at all. There was not the
5 slightest sign that it was alive. It was quite stiff. Gibberne
held it by the neck. It was like running with a dog of
wood. 'Gibberne,' I cried, 'put it down!' Then I said
something else. 'If you run like that, Gibberne,' I cried,
'your clothes will start burning. Your trousers are turning
10 brown now!'

He put his hand on his trousers and stood hesitating. 'Gibberne,' I cried, coming up to him, 'put it down. This heat is too much! It's because we've been running. Two or three miles a second! Friction of the air!'

'What?' he said, glancing at the dog.

'Friction of the air,' I shouted. 'Friction of the air. Going too fast. Too hot. And Gibberne! Gibberne! I'm feeling strange. I can see people moving slightly. I believe the stuff is losing its effect. Put that dog down.'

'Eh?' he said.

'It's losing its effect!' I repeated. 'We're too hot and the stuff's losing its effect!'

He stared at me, then at the band. It's sound was certainly getting faster. Then he lifted the dog high in the air and threw it from him with all his strength. It went spinning through the air, still seeming dead, and hung at last over the sunshades of a group of laughing people. Gibberne had seized my arm. 'You're right,' he said. 'It's losing its effect. That man's moving his handkerchief. I can see it. We must get away from here fast.'

But we could not get away fast enough. Luckily perhaps. For we might have run, and if we had run, I believe we would have burst into flames. You know, neither of us had thought of that. But before we could even begin to run, the effect of the Accelerator had ended. In the smallest part of a second, it had gone. I heard Gibberne's voice, full of fear. 'Sit down,' he said, and we sat on the grass. It turned brown from our heat. There is still burnt grass in the park where we sat down.

As we sat down, the whole picture seemed to come to life. The sounds from the band turned into music. People who were walking put their feet down, and continued on their way. Papers and flags began blowing in the wind. Voices could be heard. The man in white finished winking at the girls, and walked away. All the people sitting down moved and spoke. The whole world was alive again, and was going as fast as we were. Or, to be more accurate, we were going no faster than the rest of the world. It was like slowing down in a train when it comes into a station. Everything seemed to spin around, and for a second or two I felt sick, but that was all. And the little dog which had been hanging in the air fell straight through a lady's sunshade!

That saved us. Nobody noticed our sudden appearance, except one fat old gentleman. He was certainly surprised, and afterwards looked at us suspiciously. We started to lose our heat almost at once, although the grass beneath me was uncomfortably hot. The attention of everyone was on the dog. Even the band, for the first time in its history, played the wrong notes. They were amazed that a well-fed pet dog, which had been asleep on the grass a moment ago, should suddenly fall through a lady's sunshade. Even more amazing was the fact that the dog's coat, because of its speed in the air, seemed to be slightly burned. The noise and confusion it caused was enormous. People got up and stepped on other people. Chairs were knocked over. A policeman ran to see what was happening.

I do not know how the matter was settled. We were much too anxious to escape from the place, and to get away from the old gentleman. He was still watching us. So as soon as we were cool enough, and recovered from our confusion of mind, we stood up. Walking around the edge of the crowd, we went back towards Gibberne's house. But as we left, I heard the policeman saying to the man sitting beside the lady with the broken sunshade, 'If you didn't throw the dog, who did?' The man's angry reply could not be heard in the noise.

After the return

Our return to people who moved, and to familiar noises, had been too sudden for me to make careful observations. We had also been anxious about ourselves (our clothes were still very hot, and Gibberne's white trousers had been burned slightly brown). Indeed I really made no observations of any scientific value on that return. The bee, of course, had gone. I looked for the man on the bicycle, but he had disappeared among the traffic. The bus was driving fast along the road, full of moving, living people.

We noticed, however, that the grass under the window by which we had left the house was badly burned. And the prints our feet had made on the path seemed unusually deep.

So that was my first experience of the New Accelerator. We had been running about and doing all kinds of things in no more than a second of time. We had lived half an hour while the band had played, perhaps, a dozen notes. Its effect had been that the world had stopped for our inspection. The experience might have been a lot more unpleasant than it was, for we had certainly been foolish to leave the house. It showed that Gibberne still has much to learn before his preparation can be used safely. But there is no doubt that it works.

Since that adventure, Gibberne has been working to make it safe. I have drunk some several times without the slightest bad result. I must confess, however, that I have not gone out again after drinking it. I may mention, for example, that this story has been written while I have been in its power. I began at 6.25 p.m., and my watch is now very nearly at 6.31 p.m. It is a great advantage for a busy man to be able to work like this.

Gibberne is now working on a Retarder, which will be used to weaken the power of the Accelerator. The Retarder will, of course, have the opposite effect of the Accelerator. If it is used alone, it will make many hours of ordinary time seem like a few seconds. Anyone who drinks it will be able to remain calm in the middle of the greatest excitement. The two discoveries together must certainly make great changes in the way we live. The

Accelerator will allow us to give all our attention to a single moment of time. The Retarder, on the other hand, will allow us to live without difficulty through long periods of suffering. Perhaps I am a little too confident about the Retarder, which has not yet been discovered. But there is no doubt about the Accelerator. It will be on sale within the next few months. It will be obtainable from all chemist's shops, in small green bottles. The price will be high, but fair, when you consider what it does. Gibberne's Nervous Accelerator will be its name. He hopes to supply three kinds — ordinary, strong and extremely strong.

No doubt its use will make possible a great number of wonderful things. But like all powerful preparations it will, perhaps, be wrongly used. Crimes, for example, can easily be performed by anyone who can play with time. We have, however, discussed this question very carefully, and we have decided it does not concern us. It is a problem for the lawyers and the police. We shall manufacture and sell the Accelerator. And the result? We shall have to wait and see.

THE DOOR IN THE WALL

Wallace's story

One evening, less than three months ago, Lionel Wallace told me the story of the door in the wall. He trusted me with this secret of his, and I am certain that he believed it was true. He told it so sincerely that, at the time, I found *5*
it hard not to believe him.

When I awoke the next morning, however, I felt differently. As I lay in bed, I remembered the things he had said. I experienced again the charm of his slow, serious voice. I saw the gleaming dinner-table lit by the *10*
light of a single lamp. While I was seated at it, in a room full of shadows, I had found it easy to forget the real world outside. But now, in daylight, and in my own bedroom, I thought his story could not possibly be true. 'He told it to entertain me,' I said to myself. 'He invented a mystery *15*
to puzzle me. How well he did it!' But then I thought, 'He isn't the kind of person you would expect to make up imaginary stories.' I tried to explain to myself too, why the impossible events in the story had seemed so real. Perhaps some of the things may have happened to him. *20*
And perhaps he put them together in a story, because that was the only way he could talk about them.

Well, that is not the explanation I would give now. I am no longer uncertain. I believe now what I believed when Wallace first told me the story. He had a secret, and *25*
he did his very best to reveal it to me. But I am completely unable to say whether he saw the things he talked about or only thought he saw them. I do not know whether he really had the power to see beyond the real world, or whether he was the victim of a strange and wonderful *30*

dream. Even the fact that he is dead, which made me believe his story, does not give us an answer. That is something the reader must decide for himself.

I forget exactly why he chose to tell his secret to me. I think he was defending himself against something I had written about him. His ideas on an affair of public importance had disappointed me, and I had suggested they had been carelessly worked out. We met at dinner to discuss them, and although normally he spoke little, he started talking immediately. 'There is something,' he said, 'which is troubling me!'

'I know,' he continued, after a pause, 'I have been careless. The fact is — it is not a case of ghosts or devils — but — it's a strange thing to say, Redmond — there is something I can't stop thinking about. It interferes with my understanding of things. It excites me with strange desires.'

He stopped. Like many Englishmen, he had difficulty in talking about things that were serious, or beautiful, or concerned his feelings. 'Well — ' and he stopped again. Then, hesitating at first, but afterwards speaking more easily, he began his story. And he told me of a memory of beauty and happiness that had been with him all his life. How it filled his heart with desires that could never be satisfied. And how it made all the interests and events of this world seem dull, empty and vain.

Now that I know the facts, I remember that his face seemed to show what was wrong with him. I have a photograph in which he looks like someone who is troubled by strange thoughts; someone with an interest in things outside this life of ours. And yet, when he gave his attention to the affairs of this world, Wallace was a very successful man. He was much more successful than I was, and more famous than I would ever be. He was not yet forty and they say that, if he had lived, he might have held the highest post in the government. At school, he always beat me without effort. He was confident of his ability to be first in everything. And although I usually did rather well, he always did better. It was at our school that I had heard of the door in the wall for the first time. I heard of it the second time a month before his death.

To him, the door in the wall was real, and it led through a real wall to things which really were there. I am quite sure of that now.

And it came into his life quite early, when he was a child of five or six. 'There was a white wall,' he said slowly, 'standing in the clear yellow sunlight. And outside the green door, there were leaves on the pavement. They were yellow and green in colour, not brown and dirty, so they must have just fallen. That means it was October, and I was five years and four months old.'

He was, he said, a rather clever little boy. He had learned to walk at a very early age, and he was such a sensible child that he was allowed a great deal of freedom. After the death of his mother, he had his own private teacher. She was less strict, and looked after him less carefully. His father was a lawyer. He was a stern man, interested only in his work. Although he gave his son little attention, he expected him to grow up to be a great man. I believe that, in spite of his cleverness, young Wallace found life lonely and dull. And one day he wandered off on his own.

He could not remember how he managed to get away from home. Nor could he remember the West London

roads he walked along. All that was forgotten. But he
remembered the white wall and the green door quite
clearly.

He remembered that, at the first sight of the door, he
5 had a strange desire to go to it, open it, and walk in. At
the same time, he felt that this would be unwise, and that
it would be wrong to yield to this desire. He said he was
sure that he knew from the very beginning that the door
was unlocked, and that he could go in if he wanted to.

10 I seem to see the little boy standing there, attracted to
the door, tempted by it, but at the same time afraid of it.
And he was quite certain, though he never explained why,
that to enter it would make his father angry.

Wallace described very clearly the moments in which
15 he hesitated. He went past the door, stopped, put his
hands in his pockets, started to whistle, and then walked,
still whistling, along the street. He reached the end of the
wall, and saw some shabby, dirty shops. He particularly
remembered a painter's shop with its untidy tins of paint.
20 He stood pretending to look at these things with interest,
while all the time he was fighting the desire to enter the
green door.

Suddenly he turned and ran. There was no hesitating
this time. He went through the green door, his hands
25 stretched out in front of him. It closed behind him with a
bang, and he was in the garden he would remember all
his life.

Wallace found it difficult to describe the garden to me,
and how he felt after he was inside it.

30 ## The happy garden

There was something in the air that he breathed there,
that filled him with joy and excitement. He felt happier,
his troubles left him. The garden seemed to be a place
where only good things happened. All its colours were
35 clear and perfect. It gave him an enormous feeling of

gladness, a rare feeling only possible when one is young
and joyful. And everything was beautiful there.

Wallace thought a moment before he continued. 'You
see,' he said, in the voice of a man telling of things he
can hardly believe, 'there were two great panthers there. 5
Yes, spotted panthers. And I was not afraid. There was a
long white path with flowers along both its sides. And
these two huge beasts, with skins as soft and smooth as
silk, were playing with a ball, just like a pair of kittens.
One looked up and came towards me. It came close to 10
me and rubbed its soft, round ear very gently against the
small hand I held out. There was, I tell you, magic in that
garden. I know. And the size. Oh! It was enormous. There
were hills far away. I don't know where London had gone
to. And somehow it was just like coming home. 15

'Do you know that as soon as the door closed behind
me, I forgot the road with its fallen autumn leaves,
its carts, and its shopkeepers? I forgot the
strict rules and obedience I had learned
at home. I forgot all uncertainties

and fears, forgot all worries, forgot all the familiar facts of this life. I became in a moment a very glad and happy little boy, full of wonder, in another world. It was a different kind of world. Its light was warmer, clearer, more
5 gentle. There was a faint sense of pure gladness in its air. In the blue sky above it, floated a few, high, sunlit clouds. And before me ran a long, wide path, with charming gardens on both sides, full of flowers. And there were these two great panthers. I put my little hands fearlessly
10 on their soft fur, and gently stroked their ears, and played with them. They seemed to be welcoming me home. I had, indeed, a strong feeling that I had come home.

'And when presently a tall, beautiful girl appeared on the path, and came to me smiling, and said, "Well?" I felt
15 no amazement. When she lifted me, and kissed me, and put me down, this seemed to me perfectly and delightfully normal. I was reminded of happy things that had, in some strange way, become forgotten. The girl led me by the hand to some broad, red steps. We could see them
20 between rows of tall, blue flowers. We went up the steps onto a great avenue, between very old and shady trees. Along this avenue were seats and statues of stone, and some very tame and friendly white birds.

'My friend led me along this cool avenue. I remember
25 her sweet, kind face as she looked down at me, and asked me questions in a soft, pleasant voice. And she told me things that I know were pleasant, although I can never remember them. Presently a monkey came down a tree and ran beside us, looking up at me happily. It had clean
30 brown fur and kind eyes, and soon it jumped on my shoulder. So the two of us continued our walk in great happiness.' He paused.

'Yes?' I said, wanting him to tell me more.

'I remember little things. We passed an old man, in deep
35 thought amongst the trees, and a place made gay with bright, coloured birds. We came to a wide, cool palace, full of pleasant fountains, and all kinds of beautiful things.

It seemed a place in which there was all I would ever desire. And there were many things, and many people. I can see some clearly, others less clearly, but all the people were beautiful and kind. Somehow I understood they were all glad to see me there. They were all kind to me, and the touch of their hands, and the welcome and love in their eyes, filled me with gladness.'

The dark woman

He thought for a while. 'I found children I could play with there. This made me glad, because I was a lonely little boy. They played the most delightful games on the grass amongst the flower gardens. And while we played, we loved …

'But — it's strange — there's something missing in my memory. I don't remember the games we played. I never remembered. Afterwards, as a child, I often cried as I tried to remember. But I never succeeded. I wanted to play again the games that had made me so happy, but they were forgotten. All I remember is the happiness of the two dear children who played with me the most …

'Then presently a rather sad, dark woman, with a solemn, pale face, and dreamy eyes came to me. She wore a long, soft dress of pale purple, and carried a book. She made me follow her to a long room above a hall. The other children were unwilling to let me go. They stopped playing, and stood and watched as I was taken away. "Come back to us!" they cried. "Come back to us soon!" I looked up at her face, but she paid no attention to them. Her face was very gentle and solemn. She led me to a seat in the room, and I stood beside her. I was ready to look at her book when she opened it on her knee. The pages were turned. She pointed, and I looked. Wonder filled me, for in the living pages of that book, I saw myself. It was a story about myself, and in it were all the things that had happened to me since I was born …

'It was wonderful to me, because the pages of that book
were not pictures, you understand, they were real.'

Wallace stopped, and looked at me uncertainly.

'You mean they were moving — like looking through
5 a window,' I said. 'Please go on.'

'They were real — they must have been. Real people
moved, and real things came and went in them. I saw my
dear mother whom I had nearly forgotten, my father, tall
and solemn, the servants, my own room, and all the
10 familiar things of home. Then the front door of our house
appeared, and the busy streets filled with people. I looked
and wondered, and then looked uncertainly into the
woman's face. I turned the pages, missing some here and
there, because I was anxious to see as many as possible.
15 And so, at last, I came to a picture, and saw myself
hesitating outside the green door in the long white wall.
And I felt again the uncertainty and the fear.

'"And the next one?" I cried, and would have turned
more, if the cool hand of the solemn woman had not
20 stopped me

'"Next?" I insisted, and struggled gently with her hand.
I pulled up her fingers with all my childish strength. She
yielded and the page turned. As it moved, she bent over
me like a shadow and kissed my cheek.'

25 **The sad return**

'But the page did not show the garden, nor the panthers,
nor the girl who had led me by the hand. Nor did it show
the children who had played with me, and been so
unwilling to let me go. It showed a long grey street in
30 London, in that cold hour of the afternoon before the
lamps are lit. And I was there, small and miserable. I was
crying because I could not return to the friends I had
played with, the children who had called "Come back to
us! Come back to us soon!" But this was no page in a
35 book. I was there. It was real, cruelly real. That delightful

garden, the gentle hand of the mother I had stood beside, had gone. Where had they gone?'

He stopped again, and remained for a time staring into the fire.

'Oh! The sadness of that return!' he whispered.   5

'Well?' I said, after a minute or two.

'How miserable I felt, when I was brought back to this grey world again! When I realized fully what had happened to me, I was unable to control my sorrow. I can still remember the shame of crying in public, and the   10
disgrace of my return home. I see again the kind-looking old gentleman, who stopped and spoke to me. Touching me with his umbrella, he said, "Poor little boy. Are you lost then?" Me — a London boy, five years old or more — lost! And he insisted on fetching a kindly young policeman, and we all marched home together. Ashamed and frightened, and with tears still in my eyes, I came back from the magic garden, to the steps of my father's house.

'Those are my memories of the garden — memories which have never left me. Of course, it is impossible to describe fully the special quality of that garden. It was so different from the ordinary world. It was like a dream. And if it was a dream, I am sure it was a day-dream, and a quite extraordinary day-dream.

'Naturally everyone asked me questions — my aunt, my   35
father, the nurse, the teacher — everyone. I tried to tell them, and my father gave me my first beating for telling

lies. When I tried to tell my aunt, she punished me again
for the same thing. Then, as I said, no one was allowed
to listen to me, to hear a word about it. Even my books
of fairy stories were taken from me for some time, because
5   I had too much imagination! My father had old-fashioned
ideas. And since no one would listen, I began to repeat
the story to myself. I whispered it to my pillow, which
was often wet with childish tears. And I always added to
my usual prayers this eager wish: "Please God, may I
10   dream of the garden! Oh! Take me back to my garden!
Take me back to my garden!"

'I often dreamt of the garden. I may have changed the
facts about it. I may have added to them. I do not know.
All this, you understand, is an attempt to tell a story from
15   the confused memories of a very early experience. After
that, there is an empty space between my memories of
the garden, and those of my later boyhood. There was a
time when it seemed impossible that I should ever speak
of that wonderful sight again.'

20   I asked him if he had ever tried to return.

'No,' he said, 'I don't remember ever trying to find my
way back to the garden in those early years. This seems
strange to me now. Probably it was because my
movements were carefully watched. They did not want to
25   let me wander away again. No, it wasn't until you knew
me that I tried to go to the garden again. And I think that
for a time, although now it seems difficult to believe, I
forgot the garden completely. That may have been when
I was about eight or nine. Do you remember when I was
30   a boy at Saint Athelstan's?'

'Of course!'

'I didn't seem to have a secret dream then, did I?'

The second time

Suddenly he looked up and smiled.

35   'Did you ever play North-West Passage with me? No, of
course, you didn't come to school my way!

'It was the sort of game,' he said, 'that every child with imagination plays all day. The idea was to discover a North-West Passage to school. The way to school was plain enough. The game was to find some way that wasn't plain. I would start walking in the wrong direction ten minutes early, and then find my way to school along unfamiliar streets. And one day I got lost among some rather poor streets, on the other side of a hill near my home. I began to think I would arrive at school late and, for the first time, lose the game. I went down a street at the end of which there was a narrow lane. I hurried along this hopefully. "I shall get there yet," I said, and passed some shabby shops, that were somehow familiar to me. Suddenly, there it was! The long white wall and the green door, that led to the magic garden! I realized, then, that the garden, the wonderful garden, wasn't a dream!'

He stopped.

'I suppose my second experience with the green door shows the difference between the child's life, and the schoolboy's. The child has plenty of free time. The schoolboy is too busy to have any. However, this second time, I never thought of going in immediately. You understand — I wanted to get to school in time, and this idea completely filled my mind. I must have felt a small desire to try to open the door. Yes, I must have felt that. But it seemed to me, that the attraction of the door might prevent me from getting to school in time. I was extremely interested in the discovery I had made, of course. My mind was full of it. But I was determined to arrive at school on time, and so I continued my journey. It didn't stop me. I ran past it, and I started going down the hill, into streets that I knew well. I arrived at school, short of breath, and wet with sweat, but I was in time. I can remember hanging up my coat and hat. I went straight past that door, and left it behind me. Strange, eh?'

He looked at me thoughtfully. 'Of course I didn't know then that it wouldn't always be there. Schoolboys have imperfect imaginations. It was nice to have found it again. And I suppose I thought I could find my way back. But I had to do my school-work. I expect I was rather excited and careless that morning, as I thought of the beautiful, strange people I should presently see again. Curiously enough, I had no doubt in my mind that they would be glad to see me. Yes, that is how I must have thought of the garden that morning. It seemed a nice place which I could visit sometimes when I wasn't studying.

'I didn't go that day at all, perhaps because I knew the next day was a half-holiday. Perhaps, too, I was given extra work as punishment for not paying attention. This would have prevented me from finding time for the longer journey home. I don't know. But I do know that the garden filled my mind so completely that I had to tell someone about it.'

Wallace tells his secret

'I told — what was his name? A boy we used to call Squiff.'

'Young Hopkins,' I said.

'Yes, Hopkins. I did not like telling him. I had a feeling that telling him was somehow against the rules. But I told him. He went part of the way home with me. He always liked talking. If we had not talked about the magic garden, we would have talked about something else. And so, because the garden was the only thing I could think of, I told my story.

'Well, he revealed my secret. The next day, at playtime, half a dozen bigger boys surrounded me. They joked about my story, but at the same time they wanted to know more about the garden. There was big Fawcett — you remember him? And Carnaby, and Morley Reynolds. You weren't there, were you? No, I should have remembered if you had been.

'A boy is a creature with strange feelings. I hated myself because I had told my secret. Yet I was also pleased by the attention of those older boys. I particularly remember one moment. Crawshaw — you remember, the composer's son — said it was the best lie he had ever heard. This gave me great pleasure. But at the same time, mixed with the pleasure, there was a painful feeling of shame. I felt I had told a very special secret. That beast Fawcett made a joke about the girl — '

Wallace's voice became unhappy as he remembered the shame. 'I pretended not to hear,' he said. 'Well, then Carnaby suddenly called me a young liar. He disagreed with me when I said it was true. I said I knew where to find the green door. In ten minutes, I could lead them all there. Carnaby then said I'd have to do so — or suffer punishment. Did Carnaby ever twist your arm? Then perhaps you'll understand how I felt. I swore my story was true. There was nobody in school who could save me from Carnaby, although Crawshaw tried. Carnaby had found another victim. I became excited, and a little frightened. I behaved like a silly little boy. And the result was that I did not first go alone to find the garden. Instead, with my cheeks red, my ears hot, and tears in my eyes, I went with a group of six joking and curious schoolboys.

'We never found the white wall and the green door ...'

'You mean — ?'

'I mean I couldn't find it. I would have found it if I could. And afterwards, when I went alone, I couldn't find it. I seem now to have been always looking for it during my school-days, but I never found it — never!'

'Did the other students — make it unpleasant?'

'Terrible! Carnaby held a meeting and accused me of being a liar. I remember how I crept home and ran upstairs to hide my tears. When I fell asleep that night, I was crying, but it wasn't because of Carnaby. It was because of the garden, and the beautiful afternoon I had hoped for. I wanted to meet the sweet, friendly woman again, and play that beautiful forgotten game.

'I believe firmly that if I had not told anyone, I may have found it. I had bad times after that. I cried at night, and my mind wandered by day. I did no hard work for two terms and had very bad reports. Do you remember? Of course you do! It was you — you beat me in mathematics, and made me start working again.'

The third time

For a time, my friend stared silently into the fire. Then he said, 'I never saw it again until I was seventeen.

'I was in our car being driven to the station. I was on my way to catch a train to Oxford, where I was trying to get a place at the university. Confident of success, and feeling pleased with myself, I was looking out of the window, and suddenly there was the door, the wall, and the memory of the unforgettable things behind them.

'We drove past. I was too surprised to do anything until we were round the corner. Then came a strange moment. I knew it was still possible for me to visit the garden. I asked the driver to stop. "Yes, sir!" he said. I looked at my watch. "Er — well — it's nothing," I cried. "My mistake! We haven't much time. Go on!" And he went on.

'I got my place at the university. And the night after I was told of my success, I sat by the fire in my little upper room. I thought of the rare praise and the wise advice my father had given me. And then, smoking my favourite pipe, I thought of the door in the wall. "If I had stopped," I thought, "I would have missed the university. I would have missed my meeting with the professor. I would not have been admitted. My future would have been spoiled! I am beginning to understand things better!" I was sure that for my future's sake, it was right to give up the happiness of the garden.

'Those dear friends, and the clear air of the garden, seemed very sweet to me, but far away. My interest now was in the affairs of this world. I saw another door opening — the door of my future profession.'

He stared again into the fire. In its light I saw, for a moment, the firm strength of his face. And then it disappeared.

'Well,' he said, and sighed, 'I have worked hard at my profession. I have been successful, and there have been years of hard work when I never saw the door. This world offered so many interests and opportunities. But with that has come a feeling of disappointment with my life. Recently I began to think it sad that I should never see the door again. Perhaps I was working too hard. Perhaps I was becoming too old. I don't know. But certainly, life seemed more difficult, and the rewards of success seemed to be worthless. Strange, isn't it? And I began, a little while ago, to want the garden again, very much. Yes — and now I've seen it three times.'

'The garden?'

'No — the door! And I haven't gone in!'

He leaned over the table to me, and spoke with an enormous sorrow in his voice. 'Three times I have had my chance — three times! I swore that if I saw the door again, I would go in. I would leave the dust and heat of this world, its useless work, its worthless rewards, and never return. I swore I would go in, but when the time came, I didn't.'

Three other chances

'Three times in the last year I have passed that door, and not entered. Three times in the last year.

'The first time, Hotchkiss and I were dining with my cousin, when we were called urgently to the House of Commons to vote. We set off at once in my cousin's car. We would arrive just in time. On the way, we passed my wall and the door. I saw them clearly in the moonlight, lit by the yellow lights of our car. "My God!" I cried. "What?" said Hotchkiss. "Nothing!" I answered, and then we were past them. I could not have stopped then. It was necessary for me to go to the House of Commons that night. The vote was of the greatest importance for the future of the country.

'And the next occasion was as I rushed to my father's house to say goodbye forever to that stern old man. At that time too, the demands of this world had to be obeyed. But the third time was different. It happened a week ago, and I remember it with shame. I had been having dinner with Gurker and Ralphs. Afterwards we talked in secret of my place in the new government. I was anxious to get a firm promise from Gurker, but I knew he could not give me one as long as Ralphs was there. The inability of that man to keep a secret, and his jealousy of me, are well known. We left the restaurant together to return home. I knew that Ralphs would have to leave us first, and I was certain that after he had gone, Gurker would make his promise. Then the ambition of my life would be reached. Just at that moment, I realized that we were walking beside the white wall, and that there before my eyes, was the green door.

'We passed it, talking. I passed it. In my mind's eye I can still see our three shadows on the wall, as we walked slowly past.

'I passed within twenty inches of that door. "If I say goodnight to them, and go in," I asked myself, "what will happen? *Amazing disappearance of famous politician*! That's what the newspapers will say." That made me hesitate. And I was anxious to hear what Gurker had to offer. And many other selfish thoughts made me wait.'

Then he turned to me with a sorrowful smile, and said slowly, 'Here I am. Still here, and my chance has gone from me. I have been offered the door three times in one year — the door that leads into a place of peace, delight, beauty and kindness, that no man on earth can ever know. ₅ And I have refused it, Redmond, and it has gone — '

'How do you know?'

'I know. I know. I am left now to do the work that prevented me from entering when I had the opportunity. You say I have success — this troublesome, worthless, ₁₀ envied thing. I have it!' He took a cigarette in his strong fingers. 'If this were my success,' he said, and crushed it, holding it out for me to see.

'Let me tell you something, Redmond. The loss is destroying me. For two months I have done no work at ₁₅ all, except the most urgent and necessary duties. My soul is full of regrets and unsatisfied desires. At night — when it is less likely I shall be recognized — I go out. I wander about. Yes. I wonder what people would think if they knew. A minister of the government, the chief of one of ₂₀ its most important departments, wandering about the town alone at night, looking for a door to a garden!'

Wallace's death

I can see now his rather pale face, the unfamiliar sorrow in his eyes. I see him very clearly tonight. I remember his ₂₅ words, the sound of his voice, and last evening's newspaper still lies on my floor, containing the news of his death. At lunch at the club today, no one talked of anything else.

They found his body very early yesterday morning, in ₃₀ a deep hole near the underground railway station. It is one of two which have been dug to prepare for extending the railway to the south. It is protected by a wooden wall built along the road. In the wall there is a small door for the workmen to enter and leave by. This door was ₃₅ accidentally left unfastened, and last night he went through it.

My mind is full of unanswered questions.

He must have walked all the way from the House of Commons that night — recently he has often walked home. I seem to see his dark form coming along the empty streets, wrapped in his thick coat, deep in thought. And then did the pale electric lights near the station cheat him? Did they make the rough wooden boards of the wall appear white? Did that unfastened door awaken some memory?

Was there ever any green door in the wall at all?

I do not know. I have told the story that he told me. There are times when I think that Wallace was merely the victim of an unfortunate accident. But that is not what I really believe. You may think me foolish if you want, but I am more than half certain that he had an unusual ability to escape, in his mind, from this world into another one, far more beautiful. The way into that beautiful world was through the door in the wall. This door existed so strongly in his imagination that it became real for him. But in the end, you will say, it deceived him, and he became its victim. But was he deceived? Here we come to the mystery that surrounds dreamers like him, these men with imagination and ideas. We are satisfied with our world, and see it as a pleasant and ordinary place. By our everyday standards, to leave it means to walk out of safety into darkness, danger and death.

But did leaving it mean that to him?

THE PURPLE PILEUS

Mr Coombes, Mrs Coombes and Jennie

Mr Coombes felt sick. The thought of his own existence, and of everyone else's, disgusted him. He walked away from his unhappy home and, to avoid the town, went down the lane. Crossing the wooden bridge over the stream, he was soon alone in the damp and silent woods. He would not allow it to continue any longer, he thought to himself. And when he was sure that no one could see or hear him, he swore aloud that he would not allow it to continue.

Mr Coombes did not swear often. He was a pale-faced little man, with dark eyes, and a thin and very black moustache. He wore a very stiff collar that had been worn many times before. His coat, although it had been good once, was now shabby. There were small holes in the fingers of his gloves. In the happy days of the past — that is, before he got married — he had looked, said his wife, like some noble lord. But now she called him — and it seems unbelievable that a wife would say this about her husband — a little worm! And this wasn't the only thing she called him, either.

They had quarrelled about that stupid girl, Jennie, again. Jennie was his wife's friend. Every Sunday, uninvited by Mr Coombes, Jennie came to lunch. And afterwards, for the whole of the afternoon, she made a lot of noise. She was a big girl with a loud voice and a louder laugh. She wore clothes that most people would have thought too brightly coloured. This Sunday she had not only come uninvited herself, but she had brought a friend with her. This was a young man as loud and brightly

dressed as herself. And Mr Coombes, in his stiff, clean collar and Sunday suit, had sat at his own table silently. He had listened angrily while his wife and her guests had talked foolishly and laughed loudly. He had made no
5 objection. And after lunch (which, as usual, was late), what did Miss Jennie do? She went to the piano and started to play noisy, popular songs! On a Sunday — the one day of the week when Mr Coombes and his neighbours tried to behave especially quietly and respectably! Now his
10 neighbours would hear her! All the people in the street would hear her! He would be respectable no longer. His reputation would be lost. He had to speak.

He had felt himself become pale and, when he tried to speak, he had seemed to have difficulty breathing. He had
15 been sitting on one of the chairs by the window — the new guest was in the most comfortable chair. He turned his head. 'Sunday!' he said over his shoulder. He spoke like a man giving a warning. 'Sunday!' His voice now sounded quite nasty.

20 Jennie had continued playing. His wife, however, had stared at him. She had been looking at some song-books piled on top of the piano. 'What's wrong now?' she said. 'Can't people enjoy themselves?'

'I don't object to sensible enjoyment,' said little
25 Coombes, 'but I won't allow week-day tunes to be played on Sundays in this house.'

Jennie stopped playing and turned clumsily round on the piano-stool. 'What's wrong with my playing now?' she said.

30 ## The quarrel

Coombes realized there was going to be a quarrel. And, as small, nervous men all over the world often do, he started too eagerly, with too strong an insult. 'Be careful with that piano-stool,' he said. 'It wasn't made for
35 elephants.'

'What do you mean, elephants?' said Jennie, angrily.
'And what were you saying about my playing, when you
knew I couldn't hear you?'

'Surely you don't object to a little music on Sundays,
Mr Coombes?' said the new guest.

Leaning back in his chair, he blew out a cloud of
cigarette smoke, and smiled in a pitying way. And at the
same time, his wife said to Jennie, 'Never mind him. Play
some more, Jennie.'

'I do,' said Mr Coombes, speaking to the new guest.

'May I ask why?' said the new guest. He was clearly not
only enjoying his cigarette, but looking forward to an
argument. Mr Coombes looked for a moment at the tall,
thin young man, dressed in a light brown suit and silver-
coloured tie. 'It would have been better manners to have
worn a black suit,' he thought. Then he replied, 'Because
it isn't good for my reputation. I'm a businessman. I have
to be careful how I behave. Sensible enjoyment — '

'His reputation!' said Mrs Coombes nastily. 'That's what
he's always saying. We've got to do this, and we've got
to do that, because of his repu — '

'If you don't care about my reputation,' said
Mr Coombes, 'why did you marry me?'

'I wonder,' said Jennie and turned back to the piano.

'I never saw such a man as you,' said Mrs Coombes.
'You've changed completely since we were married.'

Then Jennie began to play again.

'Look here!' said Mr Coombes. He could control his
temper no longer, and shouted, 'I tell you, I don't want
you to do that.' He seemed to swell with anger.

'No violence now,' said the young man in the light
brown suit, sitting up.

'And who do you think you are?' said Mr Coombes
fiercely. 'This is my house, and you don't tell me how to
behave in it.'

And then they all began talking at once. The new guest
said he was Jennie's boyfriend and intended to protect

her. Mr Coombes said he could do this anywhere except in his (Mr Coombes's) house. And Mrs Coombes said he ought to be ashamed of insulting his guests, and (as I have already mentioned) that he was a nasty little worm. In the end, Mr Coombes ordered the visitors to leave his house. When they refused to go, he said he would go himself. With a red face and angry tears in his eyes, he went outside the room. While he struggled to put on his coat, and looked around for his hat, Jennie began to play the piano again. He banged the front door so hard the house trembled, and he heard the insulting tum, tum, tum of the piano follow him into the street.

This, then, is what had made his temper so bad. And you will perhaps begin to understand why he was disgusted with his existence.

Coombes's unhappy marriage

Now he walked along the muddy path under the trees. It was late in October, and brightly-coloured fungi grew in the ditches and on heaps of leaves. The history of his marriage was a sad one, but, as he thought about it, not unusual. He now understood clearly that his wife had married him from natural curiosity, and in order to escape the work of the factory. She was much too stupid to realize it was her duty to help her husband in his business. She was greedy for enjoyment, never stopped talking, and loved parties. She was clearly disappointed to find that being married did not mean the same as being rich. Her husband's worries only annoyed her, and if he made even

the slightest attempt to control her behaviour, she
complained endlessly. Why couldn't he be nice — as he
used to be? And Coombes was such a harmless little man,
too. His only ambition was to earn enough to live on.

Then Jennie appeared, a sort of female devil. She was   5
always talking about her boyfriends and wanting his wife
to go to theatres and parties. And there were also his
wife's aunts, and cousins (male and female), who
borrowed money from him, said unpleasant things to him,
disturbed his business, annoyed good customers, and   10
generally spoiled his life. This was certainly not the first
time he had left his house in anger. Nor the first time he
had sworn fiercely, and even aloud, that 'he would not
allow it,' until his great anger was finished. This made him
feel better, but, of course, it did not solve the problem.   15
But he had never before been quite so disgusted with his
life as on this particular Sunday afternoon. The Sunday
lunch and the grey sky together combined to make him
feel there was no hope left. Perhaps too, he was beginning
to realize that, as a result of his marriage, he might fail as   20
a businessman. Soon he would be unable to pay his bills,
and after that — perhaps she might have a reason for
feeling sorry for her behaviour, when it was too late. And,
as I have already said, on the right and left of the path
through the wood, a great many different kinds of bad-   25
smelling fungi were growing.

After a time, Mr Coombes's fierce anger changed to
sadness. A small shopkeeper who has married badly is in
an unfortunate position. He needs all his money for his
business, and so cannot leave his wife, or pay her to go   30
away. His marriage must truly be for ever. Walking along
the path, Mr Coombes remembered the early days of his
marriage. He had had some money, which he had saved
for many years, and everything had seemed bright and
hopeful. And now this had happened! Was there no   35
sympathetic god to help him? It is not surprising that these
thoughts made Mr Coombes begin to consider death.

He thought of the stream he had just crossed. It should be deep enough to cover his head if he stood in the middle. And it was while he imagined himself drowning, that his eye saw the purple pileus. He looked at it for a moment without thinking, and stopped and bent to pick it up. It looked to him like a small purse. Then he saw it was the purple top of a fungus. It was a poisonous-looking purple. Its polished surface seemed wet, and it had a sour smell. He hesitated with his hand about an inch from it, and the thought of poison came into his mind. So he picked the thing, and stood up again, holding it in his hand.

The purple pileus

The smell was strong and bitter, but it was not unpleasant. He broke off a piece, and the fresh surface was pure white. In ten seconds it changed, as if by magic, to a yellowish-green colour. This new colour was not unpleasant either. He broke off two more pieces to see the change repeated. They were wonderful things, these fungi, thought Mr Coombes. And they were all, his father had told him, poisons that killed instantly. Poisons!

Why not do it here and now, thought Mr Coombes. He tasted a little piece, a very little piece indeed, a tiny piece. It was so bitter he almost spat it out again. Then it tasted merely hot. In his excitement, he swallowed it. Did he like it or not? His mind was curiously careless. He tried another bit. It really wasn't bad — it was good. His interest in the fungus made him forget his troubles. He was playing with death. He took another bite, and then slowly finished a mouthful. A curious burning feeling began in the tips of his fingers and toes. His heart began to beat faster. There was a roaring noise in his ears. He turned and looked around him, and found that his feet were unsteady. He saw and struggled towards some more of the purple fungi about a dozen yards away. He fell forward on his face, his hands stretched out towards them. But he did not eat any more of them.

Instead, he fainted.

He rolled over and sat up with a look of amazement in his face. His hat lay on the ground near him. He felt his head with his hands. Something had happened, but he could not say exactly what it was. But he no longer felt dull — he was bright and cheerful. His throat felt as if it were burning. He laughed with sudden joy. Had he been dull? He did not know, but certainly he would not be dull any longer. He got up and stood unsteadily, looking around him with a pleasant smile. He tried to remember. He could not remember very well because something seemed to be spinning inside his head. And he knew he had been nasty at home, just because they wanted to be happy. They were quite right — life should be as gay as possible. He would go home and make up the quarrel, and tell them to enjoy themselves. And why not take some of this delightful fungus for them to eat? He could fill his hat with it. Some of those red ones with the white spots as well, and a few yellow. He had been a dull dog, an enemy of happiness. He would change all that. It would be fun to turn his coat sleeves inside out, and put some flowers in his pockets. Then home — singing — for a jolly evening.

Mrs Coombes complains

After Mr Coombes left, Jennie stopped playing, and turned round on the piano-stool again. 'What a lot of excitement about nothing,' said Jennie.

5   'You know now, Mr Clarence, the trouble he gives me,' said Mrs Coombes.

'His temper is a little quick,' said Mr Clarence.

'He hasn't got the slightest sympathy with anything I do,' said Mrs Coombes, 'that's what I complain of. He
10 cares for nothing but his old shop, and if I invite any friends home, or buy a new dress or any little thing for myself, he objects. "Don't waste money," he says, "be careful what you spend," and all that. He lies awake at nights worrying about how to give me less. If I give in to
15 him once, I'm finished.'

'Of course,' said Jennie.

'If a man marries a woman,' said Mr Clarence, leaning back comfortably in the best chair, 'he must be prepared to look after her. I assure you,' he said, glancing at Jennie,
20 'I shouldn't think of marrying till I could look after my wife properly. It's complete selfishness. A man ought to have enough money, and not expect his wife — '

'I don't agree altogether with that,' said Jennie. 'I think a man should have a woman's help if he isn't mean to
25 her, you know. It's just, when a man's mean — '

'You wouldn't believe how mean he is,' said Mrs Coombes. 'But I was a fool to marry him. I might have known. If my father hadn't helped, we wouldn't even have had enough money for a proper wedding.'

30   Mr Clarence showed great surprise.

She continued, 'I wouldn't even have a woman to help me to clean the house if I didn't insist on one. And the trouble he makes about money. He comes to me almost crying, with sheets of paper and figures. "If only we can
35 last this year," he says, "the business is sure to improve." "If only we can last this year," I say, "then you'll say if

only we can last next year. I know you," I say. "And you
will make me work until I'm old and ugly. Why didn't you
marry a slave if you wanted one, instead of a respectable
girl?"'

Mrs Coombes paused for breath. But we will not listen   5
to this conversation any longer. It is enough to say that,
seated round the fire, they enjoyed their discussion of all
Mr Coombes's faults. Then, when Mrs Coombes went to
get the tea, Jennie sat on the arm of Mr Clarence's chair.
And they laughed and joked together until Mrs Coombes   10
returned. They had just moved to the round tea-table
when they heard the key being turned in the front door.

'Here's my lord,' said Mrs Coombes. 'He went out like a
mad dog, and now he's coming back like a crying puppy.'

                                                          15

Mr Coombes changes

Something fell over in the shop. It sounded like a chair.
Then there was the sound of feet dancing up the stairs.
Then the door opened and Coombes appeared. But it was
not the Coombes they knew. His torn collar hung open
round his neck. His hat, full of half-crushed fungus, was   20
held in his hands. His coat was turned inside out, and he
had bunches of yellow flowers in his
pockets. The appearance of his
clothing, however, was much less
strange than the appearance
of his face. It was coloured
blue and white.

His eyes were unusually large and bright. His pale blue
lips, slightly open, revealed his teeth. He seemed to be
smiling, but not with pleasure. 'Merry!' he said. He had
stopped dancing to open the door. 'Sensible enjoyment.
Dance.' He hopped into the middle of the room and stood
bowing.

'Jim!' screamed Mrs Coombes. Mr Clarence, his mouth
open in wonder, sat as still as a statue.

'Tea,' said Mr Coombes. 'Nice thing, tea. Fungus too.'

'He's drunk,' said Jennie in a weak voice. She had never
before seen a drunk man with such a white face, or such
large, shining eyes.

Mr Coombes held out a hand full of bright red fungus
to Mr Clarence. 'Nice stuff,' he said, 'take some.'

At that moment he was friendly. Then, when he saw
the amazement on their faces, his own expression
changed to one of terrible anger. And suddenly he seemed
to remember the quarrel which had made him leave the
house. In a voice louder than Mrs Coombes had ever
heard before, he roared, 'My house. I'm master here. Eat
what I give you!' He seemed able to make this terrible
noise without effort, as he stood holding out the fungus.

Clarence was shown to be a coward. He could not face
the anger in Coombes's eyes. He stood up, pushed back
his chair, and, keeping his head down, turned away.
Mr Coombes rushed at him. Jennie gave a little scream,
and took the opportunity to run to the door. Mrs Coombes
followed her. Clarence tried to escape. The tea-table
crashed to the ground as Coombes seized him by the
collar, and tried to push the fungus into his mouth.
Clarence was happy to leave his collar behind him, and
he shot out of the door with red bits of fungus still sticking
to his face. 'Shut the door and lock him in!' cried
Mrs Coombes. She tried to close the door, but her helpers
had gone. Jennie had disappeared downstairs into the
shop, and locked the door, while Clarence had gone
quickly into the kitchen. Mr Coombes came heavily

against the door, and Mrs Coombes, finding she could not close it, ran quickly upstairs. She locked herself in the extra bedroom.

Clarence is disgraced

The merry Coombes now came back. He still held his hat full of fungus. He hesitated at the three ways, and finally chose the kitchen. Clarence, who was trying uselessly to turn the key in the lock, gave up and rushed for the back door. He was captured before he could open it. Mr Clarence is silent about what happened next. But it seems that Mr Coombes's anger had disappeared, and he was once again friendly and jolly. And as there were knives and axes lying around, Clarence sensibly decided to do nothing to annoy him, and perhaps cause a nasty accident.

It is certain that Mr Coombes was nice to Clarence. They were like old friends together. He insisted cheerfully that Clarence try the fungus and, after the friendly struggle that followed, expressed sorrow for the mess on his guest's face. It also seems that Clarence was dragged under the tap, and his face cleaned with a hard brush. Still afraid of annoying Coombes, Clarence said nothing, and indeed tried to pretend he was enjoying it. Finally, in a rather discoloured and untidy condition, he was given his coat and helped out of the back door. Mr Coombes then remembered Jennie. But Jennie had locked her door, and she remained behind it for the rest of the evening.

Mr Coombes, still feeling gay, returned to the kitchen. There he drank, or rather spilt down the front of his coat, two bottles of the wine Mrs Coombes kept in case she needed it for her health. He made cheerful noises by breaking off the necks of the bottles with his wife's dinner plates. During the early part of his drinking, he sang several merry songs. He cut his finger rather badly with one of the bottles — the only blood that flowed in this story — and after that? It would be better if we said nothing of the other events of that Sunday afternoon. But it all ended on the kitchen floor in a deep and healing sleep.

Twenty-five years later

Twenty-five years passed. It was again a Sunday afternoon in October, and again Mr Coombes walked in the quiet wood beyond the stream. He was still the same dark-eyed man with the black moustache that we met at the beginning of the story. But his face seemed a little fatter. His overcoat was new, and his hat and gloves also. He walked with his back straight and his head up. He had the look of a man who has confidence in himself. He was a master now with three assistants. Beside him walked his brother, Tom, who had just returned from Australia. He was larger than Coombes, and burned brown by the sun. They had been talking about the difficulties of their early lives, and Coombes had also been telling his brother of his business.

'Yes, it's a good business, Jim,' said his brother, Tom. 'In today's world, you're very lucky to have made it so profitable. And you're even luckier to have a wife who's so willing to help you.'

'I can tell you in secret,' said Mr Coombes, 'that she wasn't always so willing. At first I couldn't depend on her at all. Girls are funny creatures.'

'I don't understand.'

'Although it's difficult to believe now, she once wasted all my money — spent it as soon as I earned it. And we were always fighting with each other. I was too gentle with her, and loving, and she thought the business existed only to give her pleasure. My house was like a hotel. Her relatives were always here, and her girlfriends and their boyfriends. There was even singing and joking on Sundays. It was bad for business. And she showed an interest in some of the men who came here too. I tell you, Tom, I could not do what I wanted in my own home!'

'I can't believe it.'

'It's the truth. I told her her behaviour was wrong. I said, "I'm not a rich man who can take care of a wife as if she were a pet animal. I married you because I wanted a companion who would help me. You have to help me," I said, "to make the business successful." She refused to listen. "Very well," I said, "I'm a gentle man until I lose my temper, and then perhaps you'll be surprised."'

Coombes remembers that Sunday

'Well. She wouldn't listen to anything I had to say. She thought I was a worm, and worms can't get angry. And, I tell you in secret, Tom, women like her don't respect a man unless they're a little afraid of him. So I showed her that I could lose my temper. One Sunday, a girl named Jennie came to our house, with her boyfriend. My wife used to work with her. We had a little quarrel, and I came here — it was a day like this — and thought about what I should do. Then I went back and gave them a real fight.'

'You did?'

'I did. I was mad with anger. But I didn't want to hit my wife if I could avoid it. So I fought the boyfriend, just to show her what I could do. He was a big man too, but I beat him, and smashed a few things, and gave her a fright. She ran and locked herself in the extra room.'

'Well?'

'That's all. I said to her next morning, "Now you know what I'm like when I'm really angry." And I didn't have to say any more.'

'And you've been happy ever since, eh?'

'A lot happier than we were. You have got to show them who is the master. If it hadn't been for that afternoon, we'd be beggars now. And she and her family would be complaining that I was responsible. But we're all right now. And it's a very good little business, as you say.'

They continued their walk in silence. 'Women are peculiar creatures,' said his brother Tom, after a time.

'You have to deal with them firmly,' said Coombes.

'What a lot of these fungi there are around here!' said Tom presently. 'I can't understand what use they can be.'

Mr Coombes looked. 'Maybe they're sent for some wise purpose,' he said.

And that was all the thanks the purple pileus ever got from this foolish little man, whose life it had changed completely, in a few hours, one Sunday afternoon.

THE APPLE

The stranger

'I can't just throw it away!' said the man in the corner of
the railway carriage, suddenly. Mr Hinchcliff, not hearing
him clearly, looked up. He had been staring thoughtfully
at the college cap tied to his suitcase by a piece of string,   5
and thinking about his new job. Mr Hinchcliff had just
finished his studies at London University and was going
to work as a teacher at Holmwood Grammar School. The
job was a good one, and Mr Hinchcliff looked forward to
it with pleasant excitement. Now he stared across the   10
carriage at the traveller who had just spoken.

'Why not give it away?' said this person. 'Give it away!
Why not?' He was a tall man, burned almost black by the
sun. He sat with his feet on the seat in front of him, and
stared hard at his toes. There was no one else in the   15
carriage.

'Why not?' he repeated.

Mr Hinchcliff coughed.

The stranger looked up. His curious grey eyes stared at
Mr Hinchcliff without interest for perhaps a minute. Then   20
he spoke again.

'Yes,' he said slowly, 'why not? And end it.'

'I don't quite understand what you mean, I'm afraid,'
said Mr Hinchcliff, with another cough.

'You don't quite understand me?' repeated the stranger.   25
His curious eyes looked at Mr Hinchcliff, at the suitcase and the brightly-coloured cap, and returned to
Mr Hinchcliff's youthful face. Mr Hinchcliff touched his tie
nervously.

'You are a student?' asked the stranger.   30

'I was,' said Mr Hinchcliff, rather proudly, ' — of London University.'

'A student,' said the stranger. 'One who searches for knowledge.' And suddenly he took his feet off the seat
5 and put his hands on his knees. He stared at Mr Hinchcliff as if he had never seen a student before. 'Yes,' he said, pointing a finger at him. Then he rose, took his bag, placed it on the seat and unlocked it. Quite silently he took something out. It was round and wrapped in silver
10 paper which he unfolded carefully. He held it out towards Mr Hinchcliff — a small, very smooth, golden-yellow fruit.

Mr Hinchcliff's open eyes and mouth showed his amazement. He did not try to take the object. He did not even know if the stranger wanted him to take it.

15 'That,' said the mysterious stranger, speaking very slowly, 'is the apple of the Tree of Knowledge. Look at it — small and bright and wonderful. Knowledge. And I am going to give it to you.'

Mr Hinchcliff's mind took only a moment to work out
20 an explanation. 'Mad,' his brain told him, and everything became clear. Well, the best way to deal with madmen was to treat them as if they were normal.

'The apple of the Tree of Knowledge, eh!' said Mr Hinchcliff. He pretended to show great interest, and
25 leaned forward to inspect it closely. Then he looked at the stranger and asked, 'But don't you want to eat it yourself? And besides — where did you get it from?'

'It never goes bad. I have had it for three months. And it has always been as you see it now — bright and smooth
30 and ripe and wonderful.' He laid his hand on his knee, and looked at the fruit thoughtfully. Then he began to wrap it in the paper, as though he had changed his mind about giving it away.

'But where did you get it from?' repeated Mr Hinchcliff,
35 who sometimes quite enjoyed an argument. 'And how do you know that this is really the fruit of the Tree of Knowledge?'

The history of the apple

'I bought this fruit,' said the stranger, 'three months ago
— for a drink of water and a piece of bread. The man
who gave it to me — because I saved his life — was an
Armenian. Armenia! That wonderful country — the oldest
country of all. Noah's Ark is still there, you know, lost
amongst the ice and snow of Mount Ararat. This man's
village was attacked by the Kurds, but he escaped with
some others into the mountains. Up and up they went, to
the high, lonely places, where no one had ever been
before. With the fierce Kurds close behind them, they
came to a green slope among the mountain-tops. It was
covered with tall grass, with edges as sharp as knives.
They cut anyone who dared to walk in it. But because
the Kurds were so near, they had no other way to go. In
they rushed, hoping to escape, but the attempt was of no
use. Each one left behind him a path marked by his own
blood, and it was easy for their enemies to follow. Soon
no one was left alive but this Armenian and another. He
heard the screams and cries of his friends. He listened to
the sounds of the Kurds trying to find them in the grass,
which now rose above their heads. Then there was
shouting and answers, and suddenly all was
quiet. He could not understand the
stillness, so he struggled on, until
he came out of the grass on the
other side. There, standing at
the foot of a steep rocky
cliff, he looked back, and
saw that the grass was all
on fire. A cloud of smoke
rose between him
and his enemies.'

The stranger paused. 'Yes?' said Mr Hinchcliff. 'Yes? What happened next?'

'There he was, I say, all cut and bleeding from the sharp edges of the grass. The rocks were hot under the blazing sun. The afternoon sky was yellow with smoke. The fire was advancing towards him. He dared not stay there. He was not afraid of death if it came quickly, but he had no wish to die slowly and in pain. Far away beyond the smoke he heard shouts and cries, and the screaming of women. He went up the cliff, climbing among rocks and dead bushes. At last he reached a place where he was hidden from the Kurds, and there he met his friend, who had also escaped. And, fearing the Kurds more than they feared cold and hunger and thirst, they climbed up into the heights, and among the snow and ice. They wandered for three whole days.'

The strange valley

'On the third day they had a strange experience. I suppose hungry men often imagine things. But they believed that what they saw was real. Besides, there is this fruit.' He lifted the wrapped object in his hand. 'And I have heard stories like theirs from other people who have been up in those mountains. In the early evening, when the stars were beginning to shine, they came down a slope of slippery rock into a huge, dark valley. Strange, twisted trees grew all over it, and from the branches of these trees, little, round fruits hung down, glowing with a strange, yellow light.

'Suddenly the valley was lit from far away, from many miles away. The brightness came from a golden flame that marched slowly across it, and made its slopes shine with a golden light. And their own bodies shone too, amongst the black shapes of the trees. At once, they realized where they were. And because they knew the story of Eden, and of who guarded Eden, they dropped to the ground as if they were dead.

'When they dared to look up again, the valley was dark, but only for a moment. Then the light came again. The bright flame returned.

'When he saw this, the man's friend jumped to his feet. With a shout he began to run towards the light, but the man himself was too frightened to follow. Amazed and fearful, he stood watching his friend grow smaller, as he ran away from him, towards the advancing brightness.

And his friend had hardly set out when there came a noise like thunder. It was the sound of huge, unseen wings hurrying up the valley. And this sound brought with it a great and terrible fear. At this moment, the man turned and ran. If there was still time, he would try to escape. He rushed up the slope again, chased by the storm of sound. And as he climbed, he fell against one of the twisted trees, and a ripe fruit dropped from it into his hand. This fruit. The one here in my hand. And then the noise of wings and thunder was all around him. He fell and fainted.

'When he recovered, he was back amongst the burned ruins of his own village, and I and others were giving treatment to the wounded villagers. Had he only imagined these things? But he still held the golden fruit of the tree
5   tightly in his hand. Others were there who knew the story of Eden, and who knew what this strange fruit might be.' He paused. 'And this is it,' he said.

It was an unusual story to hear on a railway train in England. Mr Hinchcliff was confused. He could not decide
10   whether to believe it or not. All that he could say was, 'Is it?'

'The story of the Garden of Eden,' said the stranger, 'tells us where those strange trees came from. They grew from the apple that Adam carried in his hand, when he
15   and Eve were forced out of Eden. He felt something in his hand, saw the half eaten apple, and threw it away angrily. And now they grow in that lonely valley, for ever surrounded by snow, and for ever surrounded by swords of fire.'

20   'But I thought these things were — ' Mr Hinchcliff paused '— stories, just stories — made up long ago. Do you mean that in Armenia — ?'

The stranger answered the unfinished question by showing the fruit in his open hand.

25   'But you don't know,' said Mr Hinchcliff, 'that that is the fruit of the Tree of Knowledge. The man may have had — a sort of dream. He may have imagined it. Just suppose — '

'Look at it,' said the stranger.

30   ## The fruit of the Tree of Knowledge

It was certainly a strange-looking object. Mr Hinchcliff saw that it was not really an apple. It had a curious glowing golden colour. A light seemed to be shining from deep inside it. As he looked at it, he began to see the lonely
35   valley among the mountains, the guarding swords of fire,

the ancient details of the strange story he had just heard.
He rubbed one eye with a finger. 'But — ' he said.

'It has remained like that, smooth and juicy, for three
months — for more than three months. There has been
no drying, none at all.'   5

'And you yourself,' said Mr Hinchcliff, 'really believe
that it — '

'It is the fruit of Knowledge.' From the look on his face,
it was impossible to doubt that the traveller believed what
he said.   10

'Suppose it is?' said Mr Hinchcliff, after a pause, still
staring at it. 'But it's not my kind of knowledge — not the
sort of knowledge I mean. Adam and Eve have eaten it
already.'

'Adam and Eve have given us their sins, not their   15
knowledge,' said the stranger. 'That apple would make us
all clear and bright again. We should see through
everything, understand everything, know the deepest
meaning of everything — '

'Why don't you eat it, then?' interrupted Mr Hinchcliff. 20
He felt rather pleased with this suggestion.

'When I took it, I intended to eat it,' said the stranger.
'But the whole of mankind suffers because of the sins of
Adam and Eve. To eat the fruit again could scarcely — '

'Knowledge gives men power,' said Mr Hinchcliff.   25

'But does it bring them happiness? I am older than you
— more than twice as old. I have held this in my hand
many times, and I have lost courage when I thought of
all that I might know. How terrible to see everything so
clearly that nothing is hidden.'   30

'I think that would be a great advantage,' said
Mr Hinchcliff.

'Suppose you saw into the most secret thoughts and
feelings of everyone around you, especially of the people
you loved, and whose love you thought important to you?' 35

'You'd soon find out who was deceiving you,' said
Mr Hinchcliff, rather attracted by the idea.

'And worse, suppose you knew yourself. Suppose you saw clearly your own character, with all its faults, and understood what they prevented you from succeeding in. Suppose you could not hide any of your own weaknesses
5   from yourself.'

'That might be an excellent thing too. There's an old saying, "know yourself", you know.'

'You are young,' said the stranger.

'If you don't want to eat it, and it bothers you, why
10   don't you throw it away?'

'Once again, you do not understand me. How could I throw away a glowing, wonderful thing like that? How could anyone, after possessing it, throw it away? But, on the other hand, to give it away! To give it away to
15   someone who desired knowledge more than anything else, who was not afraid to understand things clearly —'

'Of course,' said Mr Hinchcliff thoughtfully, 'it might be some sort of poisonous fruit.'

Hinchcliff has the apple

20   At that moment, he realized the train had stopped. At the same time, he noticed outside the carriage window the end of a white board. The black letters on it spelt — MWOOD. He leapt from his seat with surprise. 'Gracious!' said Mr Hinchcliff. 'Holmwood!' And all the strange ideas
25   that had been creeping into his mind were gone instantly.

In a moment, he had opened the carriage door, his suitcase in his hand. The guard was already waving his green flag. Mr Hinchcliff jumped out. 'Here!' said a voice behind him. He turned and saw a pair of dark, shining
30   eyes. The stranger held out the bright, golden fruit through the open carriage door. Mr Hinchcliff took it without thinking. The train was already moving.

'No!' shouted the stranger, and tried to take it back again.

35   'Stand away,' cried the guard, running forward to close the door. The excited stranger put his head and arm

outside the window. He shouted something — Mr Hinchcliff did not hear. And then the shadow of the bridge covered him, and in a moment he could no longer be seen.

Mr Hinchcliff stood amazed, staring at the last carriage disappearing round the bend, and holding the wonderful fruit in his hand. For a second his mind was confused. Then he realized that two or three people on the platform were looking at him with interest. Was he not the new master of Holmwood Grammar School, making his first appearance? Hoping that they thought the fruit might be just an orange, he put it quickly in his pocket. It made a lump which stuck out from his jacket. Then, clumsily trying to hide his embarrassment, he went towards them. If it had been possible, he would have avoided them. However, he had to find out the way to the school, and how to send his luggage there. What a strange, amazing story he had heard!

He found out that a cart would take his luggage, and he could go on foot. He thought he heard amusement in the voices of the group on the platform. The lump in his pocket made him feel even more awkward.

The serious manner of the man on the train, and the strangeness and excitement of his story, had prevented Mr Hinchcliff from thinking about his job for some time. Fires that marched up and down! Now his concern for his new post filled his mind again. He wanted to gain the respect of the people of Holmwood, particularly the

people of the school. This was his main purpose, and it put all other thoughts out of his mind. But one thing still worried Mr Hinchcliff. He took great care over his appearance. And he found the small, soft, golden fruit in
5 his pocket extremely troublesome. The lump made him feel uncomfortable. It spoiled the shape of his suit. He passed a little old lady dressed in black, and he saw that she noticed the lump at once. He was wearing one glove, and carrying the other together with his stick. So it was
10 impossible to carry the fruit in his hand. He took it from his pocket in a place where the road was quiet, and put it on his head, under his hat. It was just too large. His hat became unsteady on his head when he walked, and made him look foolish. Just as he was taking the fruit out again,
15 a messenger boy came cycling round the corner, and saw what he was doing.

'Confound it!' said Mr Hinchcliff.

Only one thing prevented him from eating the fruit there and then, and so obtaining unlimited knowledge. It
20 would seem so silly, he thought, to go into the town sucking a juicy fruit — and it certainly felt juicy. If one of the schoolboys should see him, he might later have difficulty in keeping order in class. And the juice might stick to his hands and face. Or it might leave a dirty mark
25 on his clothes.

The fruit is lost

Then, coming round a bend in the lane, he saw in the sunlight two very pleasant-looking girls. They were walking slowly towards the town, talking happily. In a
30 moment they might look round, and see a hot-faced young man behind them, carrying a funny-looking shining fruit. They would be sure to laugh.

'Confound it!' said Mr Hinchcliff again, and hastily threw the troublesome object over a stone wall into a field. As
35 it went out of sight, he experienced a faint feeling of

regret, but it lasted scarcely a moment. Holding his glove and stick more firmly in his hand, he straightened his back and walked past the girls, feeling their eyes following him.

But in the darkness of the night Mr Hinchcliff had a dream, and saw the valley, and the swords of fire, and the strange, twisted trees. Then he knew that it really was the apple of the Tree of Knowledge that he had thrown so carelessly away. And he awoke feeling very unhappy.

In the morning, his regret had gone. But afterwards it often returned and troubled him, unless he was happy, or busy with his work. At last, one moonlit night at about 11.00 p.m., when all Holmwood was quiet, his regrets returned with twice as much force. With them came a desire for adventure, which he had to obey. Quietly he crept out of the house, and over the playground wall. He went through the silent town to Station Lane, and climbed into the field where he had thrown the fruit. But he did not find it. Among the damp grass, and the faint shapes of the flowers, nothing remained.

THE MAN WHO COULD WORK MIRACLES

Fotheringay works a miracle

It is uncertain if he was able to do this when he was born. I think the ability came to him later, and quite suddenly. Indeed, until he was thirty, he did not believe in miracles
5   at all. And here, since it is a suitable place, I must mention that he was a little man with brown eyes and very stiff, straight red hair. His name was George McWhirter Fotheringay and he was a clerk at Gomshott's. He was not the sort of man that you would expect miracles from. And
10 yet it was during an argument about miracles, that he first realized his own extraordinary powers. This particular argument was being held in the bar of the Long Dragon. Fotheringay had been declaring that miracles were not possible. Toddy Beamish, who believed the opposite, had
15 been arguing that they were.

Besides these two, there were, in the bar, a very dusty traveller, the landlord, Cox, and the respectable and rather fat Miss Maybridge, who worked there. Miss Maybridge was standing with her back to Mr Fotheringay, washing
20 glasses. The others were watching him, amused to see him slowly losing patience with Beamish, who refused to agree with anything he said.

'Look here, Mr Beamish,' said Mr Fotheringay, trying for the last time to persuade the man. 'Let us clearly
25 understand what a miracle is. It's something done by the will that does not obey the laws of nature.'

'That is what you say,' said Beamish. This was his favourite sentence in an argument, and it never failed to annoy Fotheringay.

He now asked the traveller, who had been listening silently, for his opinion. This gentleman, after a hesitating cough and a glance at Beamish, gave his support. The landlord, however, would not say what he thought. Mr Fotheringay, turning back to Beamish, heard him say, to his surprise, that his description of a miracle might be right.

'For example,' said Mr Fotheringay, greatly encouraged, 'this would be a miracle. That lamp couldn't burn upside down, could it? It would be against the laws of nature, wouldn't it?'

'That is what you say,' said Beamish.

'And you,' said Fotheringay, 'you don't mean to say it could burn upside-down, do you?'

Beamish hesitated and then admitted, 'No, it couldn't burn.'

'Good,' said Fotheringay. 'Now let us imagine that someone comes here, me perhaps. I say to that lamp, I command it, as I am doing now, "Turn upside-down without breaking, and carry on burning", and — hullo!'

It was enough to make anyone say 'Hullo!' The amazing, the impossible, had happened before their eyes. The lamp hung upside-down in the air, burning quietly, with its flame pointing downwards. It was there, solid and
5 real, the ordinary, common lamp of the Long Dragon bar.

Mr Fotheringay stood pointing with his finger. He looked like someone who expects a crash at any moment. The traveller, who was sitting next to the lamp, turned and jumped over a table to get away from it. Everyone
10 jumped. Miss Maybridge jumped and screamed. For nearly three seconds the lamp remained still. A faint, troubled cry came from Mr Fotheringay. 'I can't keep it up,' he said, 'any longer.' He fell back, and the lamp suddenly brightened, seemed to hesitate a moment, and then
15 smashed to the floor. Its flame stopped burning.

It was lucky it did, or the whole place would have been on fire. Mr Cox was the first to speak. What he said was simple, and not difficult to understand. Fotheringay was a fool. Fotheringay was too amazed at what had happened
20 to disagree. The conversation that followed explained nothing, but everyone agreed with Mr Cox's opinion of Fotheringay. They all accused him of playing a silly trick which had destroyed their comfort, and might have destroyed their safety. Fotheringay was too confused to
25 object to what they said. When at last they suggested that he leave, he went without defending himself.

Miracles at home

He went home feeling worried and disturbed. He watched each of the ten street lamps nervously, as he passed it. It
30 was not until he was alone in his bedroom that he was able to consider the problem seriously, and ask himself, 'What on earth happened?'

He took off his coat and shoes, and sat on the bed with his hands in his pockets. 'I didn't want it to turn upside-
35 down,' he said aloud. And then he suddenly realized that

he had wanted it. At the exact moment he had spoken
the command, his will had somehow lifted the lamp into
the air. And he had felt that he had to keep it there as
long as possible, although he didn't understand why. It
was all very confusing. He did not have a particularly
clever mind, but he soon realized the best way to settle
his confusion. He must try to do it again.

Feeling a little foolish, he pointed firmly at his candle,
and directed his thoughts towards it. 'Rise up,' he said.
The candle rose, hung in the air for a moment, and, before
Fotheringay's amazed eyes, fell on the table, leaving him
in darkness.

For a time Mr Fotheringay sat in the darkness, perfectly
still. 'It did happen, then,' he said. 'How can I explain it?
I can't.' He sighed, and began to search in his pockets for
a match. He could not find one, and rose and felt for one
on the table. 'I wish I had a match,' he said. He felt the
pockets of his coat, and there were none there. And then
he realized that miracles were possible even with matches.
He stretched out his hand and said in the dark, 'Let there
be a match in this hand.' A light object touched his fingers
and, closing them, he felt a match.

But he had no matchbox, and after several attempts to
light it, he threw the match down impatiently. And then
he realized he could use his will to light it. He did, and
the match started to burn on the table-cloth. He lifted it
hastily and put it out. Then he had another idea. He felt
for the candle, and took it in his hand. 'Here! You be lit,'
said Mr Fotheringay, and instantly the candle was burning.
By its light he saw a little black hole in the table-cloth.

His eyes moved from this to the little flame, and back
again, and then he looked up at his own face in the mirror.
For a long time he stared at it in silence.

'How about miracles now?' said Mr Fotheringay at last,
addressing his reflection.

The confusion in Mr Fotheringay's mind was now
greater than ever. But he could understand one thing. If

he wanted something to happen, it happened. Although his experiences with the lamp and candle had made him a little afraid, he decided to try one or two more harmless experiments. He lifted a sheet of paper, and turned a glass
5 of water pink, and then green. He produced a frog, which he immediately caused to disappear again, and he got himself a new toothbrush. So now he was quite sure that his will was a particularly rare and powerful one. His early experiences with it had frightened him, but now he felt
10 rather proud. And he began to understand that it might bring him a great many advantages. He heard the clock strike one and, because he still had his daily duties at Gomshott's, he began to undress, in order to go to bed. As he struggled out of his shirt, he had a wonderful idea.
15 'Let me be in bed,' he said, and he was. 'Undressed,' he said, and finding the sheets cold, added hastily, 'and in a nice, soft, woollen night-shirt. Ah,' he said, with great enjoyment, 'and now let me be comfortably asleep ...'

The flowering stick

20 He awoke at his usual hour, and was thoughtful during breakfast-time. Was his experience last night perhaps only a dream? After a time, he decided to try again some careful experiments. For example, he had three eggs for breakfast that morning. The servants supplied two. They were good,
25 but a little overcooked. The third, a fresh goose-egg, was laid, cooked, and served by his extraordinary will. He hurried off to Gomshott's, careful not to show the great excitement he felt. He only remembered the third egg when the servant spoke of the shell that night. All day
30 long he could do no work because of the amazing discovery he had made about himself. But this caused him no trouble because, by a miracle, he made up for it in his last ten minutes.

As the day passed, his state of mind changed gradually
35 from wonder to joy. It is true that he still had unpleasant

memories of the events in the Long Dragon. He would have to be careful about lifting articles that might be easily broken. However, he could use his will in many interesting ways. He decided, for example, to increase his personal possessions. He wished for a pair of diamonds, and two splendid ones appeared instantly. He made them disappear, just as quickly, when Gomshott came into the office. He was afraid he might ask how he got them. He understood quite clearly that he would have to use his power carefully and skilfully. And he understood that this would require practice. So that night, after supper, he went to a quiet path not far from his house, to try a few miracles before going to bed.

As we have said, Mr Fotheringay did not have a particularly clever mind. At first he could not think what to do. Then, seeing a stick lying at the edge of the path, he remembered a story he had once read. He picked the stick up, and stuck one end of it into the ground. Then he stepped back, and commanded it to flower. At once the air was filled with the scent of roses, and Mr Fotheringay saw that he had performed a beautiful miracle. The satisfaction he felt was ended by the sound of someone coming down the lane. He spoke hastily to the flowering stick, 'Go back.' He meant, 'Change back,' but of course he was confused. The stick moved backwards quickly. At once there was a cry of anger, and some bad language from the person in the lane.

'Who are you throwing sticks at, you fool?' cried a voice. 'That hurt my leg.'

' I am sorry,' said Mr Fotheringay. Then he saw it was Winch, one of the three village policemen, walking towards him. Realizing that an explanation would be difficult, he coughed nervously.

'Why did you do that?' asked the policeman. 'Oh! It's you, is it? The man that broke the lamp at the Long Dragon!'

'It was an accident,' said Mr Fotheringay. 'I didn't intend to do it.'

'Why did you do it, then?'

'I — I — ' said Fotheringay.

'Why did you do it?' repeated the policeman. 'Don't you know that that stick hurt? Why did you do it, eh?'

Mr Fotheringay could not think why he had done it. His silence seemed to annoy Mr Winch. 'You've attacked a policeman this time, young man. That's what you've done.'

The disappearance of Winch

'Look here, Mr Winch,' said Mr Fotheringay, still confused, 'I'm very sorry. The fact is — '

'Yes?'

He could think of nothing to say but the truth. 'I was working a miracle.' He tried to say the sentence as if he were saying something very ordinary, but he couldn't.

'Working a — ! Here, don't talk nonsense. Working a miracle indeed! Miracle! That's a joke! You're the one who doesn't believe in miracles. The fact is, this is another of your silly tricks, that's what it is. Now, I tell you — '

But Mr Fotheringay never heard what Mr Winch was going to tell him. He realized he had revealed his secret, and that the whole world would soon know about it. He experienced a feeling of great annoyance. Addressing the policeman fiercely, he said, 'Here, I've had enough of this, I have! I'll show you a silly trick, I will! You go to Hell! Go, now!'

He was alone!

Mr Fotheringay performed no more miracles that night, nor did he try to find his flowering stick. He returned to his house, frightened and very quiet, and went to his bedroom. 'Lord!' he said, 'it's a powerful thing, an extremely powerful thing. I didn't really want to do as much as that. Not really ... I wonder what Hell is like!'

He sat on the bed taking off his shoes. Then he had a happy idea, and moved the policeman to San Francisco. There was no more interference with nature that night, and he went quietly to bed. In the night, he dreamt of the anger of Police Constable Winch.

The next day Mr Fotheringay heard two interesting pieces of news. Someone had planted a most beautiful rose tree beside Mr Gomshott's private house, and they were searching in the river for Police Constable Winch.

Mr Fotheringay was thoughtful all that day. He performed only two miracles. He provided some things for Winch, which he thought he would need, and he arranged to complete his day's work at Gomshott's perfectly, and in time, in spite of all the thoughts which filled his mind. Most of these thoughts were about Winch.

On Sunday evening Fotheringay did something that he did not do often. He went to church. Strangely enough, Mr Maydig, who was interested in miracles and magic, spoke about 'things that are against the law.' Mr Fotheringay was interested in what he said. He decided to visit him later that evening, and request a private conversation.

Mr Maydig, a thin man, easily excited, with extremely long wrists and neck, was pleased to welcome Fotheringay when he arrived at his house. He led him to a comfortable room, invited him to sit down, and, standing in front of a warm fire, asked him what he wanted.

Maydig's amazement

At first Mr Fotheringay hesitated, and had difficulty in starting. 'You will hardly believe me. Mr Maydig, I am afraid — ' He talked in this way for some time, saying nothing, and then he tried a question. 'What do you think, Mr Maydig, of miracles?'

Mr Maydig was still composing his reply when Mr Fotheringay continued. 'You don't believe, I suppose, that an ordinary person — like myself, for example, sitting here now — might be able to use his will to do things.'

'It's possible,' said Mr Maydig. 'Something like that, perhaps, is possible.'

'If you have no objection, I think I can show you what I mean,' said Mr Fotheringay. 'Look at that tobacco jar on the table, for example. I want you to tell me if this is a miracle or not. Just wait a moment, Mr Maydig, please.'

He pointed to the tobacco jar and said: 'Be a vase of flowers.'

The tobacco jar did what he said.

Mr Maydig jumped when he saw the change, and stood looking from the clerk to the vase of flowers. He said nothing. Presently he leaned over the table nervously, and smelt the flowers. They had just been picked, and were very fine ones. Then he stared at Mr Fotheringay in amazement.

'How did you do that?' he asked.

Mr Fotheringay said, 'I just told it to do it — and it did it. Is that a miracle, or is it magic, or what is it? And what's the matter with me? That's what I want to know.'

'It's most amazing.'

'And last week at this time I didn't know I could do things like that. It came quite suddenly. It's something strange about my will, I suppose, and that's all I can understand.'

'Is that the only thing? Could you do other things besides that?'

'Lord, yes!' said Mr Fotheringay. 'Just anything.' He thought a moment. 'Here!' He pointed. 'Change into a bowl of fish — no, not that — change into a glass bowl full of water with fish swimming in it. That's better. You see that, Mr Maydig?'

'It's amazing. I can't believe it. You are either a most extraordinary ... But no — '

'I could change it into anything,' said Mr Fotheringay. 'Just anything. Here! Be a bluebird, will you?'

In another moment, a bluebird was flying around the room and making Mr Maydig jump nervously every time it came near him. 'Stop there now, will you?' said Mr Fotheringay. The bird remained in the air without moving. 'I could change it back into a vase of flowers,' he said. After putting the bird back on the table, he worked that miracle. 'I suppose you'll want your tobacco back,' he said. The vase became a tobacco jar.

Mr Maydig had watched all these later changes in silent amazement. He stared at Mr Fotheringay, and, rather nervously, picked up the tobacco jar, examined it, and replaced it on the table. 'Well!' was all he could say to express his feelings.

The problem of Winch

'Now, after that it's easier to explain what I came to see you about,' said Mr Fotheringay. He now started to tell the long and sometimes confused story of his strange

experiences. He began with the affair of the lamp in the Long Dragon. Mr Maydig, with the tobacco jar in his hand, listened carefully. Presently, while Mr Fotheringay was dealing with the miracle of the third egg, the minister
5 interrupted:

'It is possible,' he said. 'I believe it. It is amazing, of course, but I think I understand. The power to work miracles is a natural ability. In the past it has come only very rarely to special people. But in this case ... I have
10 always wondered ... But, of course! Yes, it is a natural ability! You have been given powers greater than the powers of nature. Yes — yes. Carry on. Carry on!'

Mr Fotheringay now told of his adventure with Winch. 'This is what has troubled me most,' said Mr Fotheringay.
15 'This is what I want advice about. Of course, he's in San Francisco — wherever San Francisco may be — but of course it's a problem for both of us, Mr Maydig. I'm sure he can't understand what's happened. And I'm sure he's afraid and very angry, and trying to get back here to me.
20 I'm sure he sets off every few hours to come back here, and I send him back, by a miracle, when I can think of it. And of course that's a thing he won't be able to understand, and that must annoy him. And, of course, if he buys a ticket every time, it will cost him a lot of money.
25 I've done the best I could for him, but he may not understand this. I thought afterwards that his clothes might have got burned, you know. If Hell is what we believe it is, they would be burnt. In that case, I suppose they put him in jail in San Francisco. Of course, I made my will
30 give him a new suit of clothes as soon as I thought of it. But, I'm already in so much trouble — '

Mr Maydig looked serious. 'I understand your difficulty. Yes, you are in a difficult position. How are you to end it ...' He talked a lot about this problem, but he had no
35 clear solution to offer.

'However,' he said after a time, 'let's forget about Winch for a few minutes and discuss the more important

question. I don't think you have been guilty of any crime.
No, none at all, unless there is something you haven't told
me. No, they're miracles — pure miracles — miracles, if
I may say so, of the very highest quality.'

He began to walk about the room, his excitement
increasing. Mr Fotheringay sat with his arm on the table
and his head on his arm, looking worried. 'I don't know
what I can do about Winch,' he said.

Mrs Minchin

'An ability to work miracles — a very great ability like
yours,' said Mr Maydig, 'will find a way to help Winch —
do not worry. My dear sir, you are a most important man,
with amazing powers. The things you may do …'

'Yes, I've thought of a thing or two I wanted to do,'
said Mr Fotheringay. 'But — some of the things didn't
work out the way I planned. You saw that fish at first? It
was the wrong sort of bowl, and the wrong sort of fish.
And I thought I'd ask someone.'

'The proper thing to do,' said Mr Maydig, 'the right thing
to do — yes, the right thing to do — ' He stopped and
looked at Mr Fotheringay. 'There seems to be no limit to
your powers. Let us test them, to see if they really are —
if they really are as great as they seem to be.'

And so, in that little room behind the church, on the
evening of Sunday, 10th November 1896, Mr Fotheringay,
encouraged by Mr Maydig, began to work miracles.

At first the miracles worked by Mr Fotheringay were
small miracles. He changed little things like cups and
furniture. He would have preferred to settle the Winch
affair first, but Mr Maydig would not let him. After they
had worked about a dozen of these miracles inside the
house, their sense of power increased, and their
imaginations and ambitions grew greater. Their first larger
miracle was the result of hunger, and the carelessness of
Mrs Minchin, Mr Maydig's servant. The meal which she

had left for him, and which he invited Mr Fotheringay to share, was a poor one. But the two busy miracle-workers were seated at the table, and Mr Maydig was describing all the faults of his servant, when Mr Fotheringay had an

5 idea. 'Don't you think, Mr Maydig,' he said, 'if you have no objection, I — '

'My dear Mr Fotheringay! Of course! No — I didn't think.'

Mr Fotheringay waved his

10 hand. 'What shall we have?' he said. At Mr Maydig's order, he changed his supper completely. 'For myself,' he said,

15 looking at Mr Maydig's choice, 'I think I'll have some mutton and red wine.' And at

20 once mutton and red wine appeared at his command. They sat long at their supper, talking like old friends. Mr Fotheringay looked forward

25 with satisfaction to all the miracles they might presently do. 'Oh, Mr Maydig,' said Mr Fotheringay, 'I might perhaps be able to help you — with your home life.'

Changing Mrs Minchin

'I don't quite understand,' said Mr Maydig, pouring himself

30 a glass of the excellent wine.

Mr Fotheringay took a mouthful of mutton. 'I was thinking,' he said, 'I might be able to work a miracle with Mrs Minchin — make her a better woman.'

Mr Maydig put down the glass, and looked uncertain.

35 'She's — she strongly objects to interference you know,

Mr Fotheringay. And — it's past eleven o'clock, and she's probably in bed and asleep. Do you think we should?'

Mr Fotheringay considered these objections. 'Why shouldn't we do it when she's asleep?'

For a time Mr Maydig argued against the idea, and then he yielded. Mr Fotheringay gave his orders, and the two gentlemen continued eating. Mr Maydig was talking about the changes he might expect in his servant next day, when confused noises began to come from upstairs. For a moment they looked at each other, and then Mr Maydig left the room hastily. Mr Fotheringay heard him calling up to his servant, and then his footsteps going softly up to her.

In a minute the minister returned, his face happy, his eyes shining. 'Wonderful!' he said. 'Wonderful!'

He began to walk about the room. 'A most wonderful change. Poor woman! A most wonderful change! She had got up. She must have got up at once. She had got up to pour away a private supply of strong drink she kept hidden in a box under her bed. And she confessed to it too! But this gives us all kinds of possibilities. If we can make this wonderful change in her …'

'The thing's unlimited, it seems,' said Fotheringay. 'And now, about Mr Winch — '

'Completely unlimited.' And standing in front of Mr Fotheringay, Mr Maydig avoided any discussion of the Winch problem, and instead made a number of suggestions, wonderful plans that he made up as he spoke.

Now what their plans were is not important to this story. It is enough to say that they were meant to help the whole of mankind. It is enough to say too, that the problem of Winch remained unsolved. Nor is it necessary to describe how these plans were carried out. There were amazing changes. Mr Maydig and Mr Fotheringay, in the early hours of the morning, were racing round the town, under the still moon, working all sorts of miracles. They improved the railway, made the parks beautiful, and cleaned up the streets. And they were going to the South Bridge to repair the damage there. 'The place,' said Mr Maydig, 'won't be the same place tomorrow. How surprised and thankful everyone will be!' And just at that moment the church clock struck three.

'That's three o'clock,' said Mr Fotheringay. 'I must go back. I've got to be at the office by eight. And besides —'

'We're only beginning,' said Mr Maydig, enjoying the feeling of unlimited power. 'We're only beginning. Think of all the good we're doing. When people wake — '

'But — ' said Mr Fotheringay.

The world stops

Mr Maydig seized his arm suddenly. His eyes were bright with excitement. 'My dear Fotheringay, there's no hurry. Look!' And he pointed to the moon high above them.

'Stop it,' he said.

'Stop it?'

'Why not? Stop it!'

'That's a little difficult,' said Fotheringay, after a pause.

'Why not?' said Mr Maydig. 'Of course it doesn't really stop. You stop the earth, you know. Then time stops. It wouldn't do anyone any harm.'

'H'm!' said Mr Fotheringay. 'Well!' He sighed. 'I'll try. Here — '

He buttoned his jacket and spoke to the world. 'Just stop turning, will you?' said Mr Fotheringay.

And it did.

Fotheringay found himself spinning wildly through the air at the rate of many miles a minute. In spite of the number of circles he was turning every moment, he was still able to think. Thought is really a wonderful thing. Sometimes it is slow, sometimes it is as quick as light. He thought in a second and shouted out, 'Let me come down to the ground safely.'

He gave his order just in time. His clothes, heated by his flying so quickly through the air, were already beginning to burn. He came down a little roughly, but without hurting himself, on what seemed to be a pile of earth. A huge lump of metal and stone hit the earth near him, and burst like a bomb. A piece of it hit a flying cow and smashed it like an egg. There was a crash which made all the most violent crashes of his past life seem like the sound of falling dust. This was followed by a number of smaller crashes. An enormous wind roared across the earth and sky so that he could hardly lift his head to look. For a while he was too amazed, even to see where he was, or what had happened.

'Lord!' said Mr Fotheringay, hardly able to speak because of the wind. 'What a fright! What's happening? Storms and thunder. And only a minute ago it was a fine night. Maydig made me do this. What a wind! If I continue with foolish tricks like this, I'm sure to have an accident. Where's Maydig? What a terrible mess everywhere!'

He looked around him. The appearance of things was really extremely strange. 'The sky's all right,' said Mr Fotheringay. And that's about all that is all right. And even there it looks as if we are going to have a terrible storm. There's the moon, up there. Just as it was a moment ago. But what about the rest — ? Where's the village? Where's — where's anything? And how did this wind start blowing? I didn't order any wind.'

Mr Fotheringay struggled uselessly to stand up and, after one failure, remained on his knees. He prevented himself from being blown away by holding on to a large piece of stone with his hands. He observed the moonlit world around him. 'There's something seriously wrong,' said Mr Fotheringay, struggling to prevent his jacket flying away. 'And what it is — I wish I knew.'

All around him nothing could be seen, in the white moonlight and in the dust blown up by the screaming wind, except heaps of earth and ruins.

There were no trees, no houses, no familiar shapes.
Destruction and disorder lay everywhere, under the
lightning and thunder of a rapidly growing storm. Near
him was something that might once have been a great
5   tree. It was smashed to pieces
from top to bottom. A
little further away was
a heap of stone and
twisted metal. Then
10   he recognized it. It
was the South Bridge.

You must understand that
when Mr Fotheringay stopped
the turning of the earth, he said nothing in
15   his command about the things on its surface. And the earth
spins so fast that, round its middle, the surface is moving
at more than 1,000 miles an hour. Further to the north and
south, it is still more than half that speed. So, when the
earth stopped moving, the village, and Mr Maydig, and
20   Mr Fotheringay, and everybody, and everything, had been
thrown violently forward at about nine miles per minute
— that is to say, much faster than if they had been shot
from a gun. And every human creature, every living
creature, every house, and every tree — all the world as
25   we know it — had thus been smashed and destroyed —
completely. Everything, everywhere. All in a matter of a
few seconds. That was all.

No more miracles

Mr Fotheringay did not, of course, fully understand these things. But he could see that the result of his miracle was not what he had intended. A feeling of great disgust with miracles came to him. He was in darkness now, for the clouds had rushed together and hidden the moon, and the air was full of rain. A great roaring of wind and water filled the earth and sky, and staring through the dust and rain in the direction of the wind, he saw, in the flashes of lightning, an enormous wall of water pouring towards him.

'Maydig!' screamed Fotheringay, in a voice which could hardly be heard in the terrible noise. 'Here, Maydig!

'Stop!' cried Mr Fotheringay to the advancing water. 'Oh, for God's sake, stop.

'Stop a moment,' said Mr Fotheringay to the lightning and thunder. 'Stop just a moment while I think ... And now what shall I do?' he said. 'What shall I do? Lord! I wish Maydig were here.

'I know,' said Mr Fotheringay. 'And for God's sake let's do it right this time.'

He remained on his hands and knees, leaning against the wind, determined to do everything right.

'Ah!' he said. 'Let nothing that I'm going to order happen until I say, "Off!" ... Lord! I wish I'd thought of that before.'

He shouted louder and louder in the wind, trying in vain to hear himself speak. 'Now then — let's start! Remember what I said just now. First of all, when I've said all I want to say, let me lose my power to do miracles. Let my will become just like anyone else's will. Let all these dangerous miracles be stopped. I don't like them. I'd rather I didn't do them. Much rather. That's the first thing. And the second is — let me be back just before that lamp turned upside-down. It's a difficult job, but it's the last. Do you understand? No more miracles —

everything as it was — me back in the Long Dragon with my drink. That's it! Yes.'

He pushed his fingers into the earth, held tightly, closed his eyes, and said, 'Off!'

5 Everything became perfectly still.

'That is what you say,' said a voice.

He opened his eyes. He was in the bar of the Long Dragon, arguing about miracles with Toddy Beamish. He had a faint feeling that some great thing had happened, 10 and been forgotten. That disappeared immediately. You understand, don't you, that, except for the loss of his powers to work miracles, everything was the same as it had been before. His mind and memory were now, therefore, the same as they had been when this story 15 began. So he knew nothing of the story that has been told here, and knows nothing of it to the present day. And among other things, of course, he still did not believe in miracles.

'I tell you that miracles can't possibly happen,' he said, 20 'and I'm prepared to prove it to you.'

'That is what you say,' said Toddy Beamish; 'prove it if you can.'

'Look here, Mr Beamish,' said Mr Fotheringay. 'Let us clearly understand what a miracle is. It's something done 25 by the will that does not obey the laws of nature … '

QUESTIONS AND ACTIVITIES

CHAPTER 1

Choose the right words to say what this part of the story is about.

On the (1) **second/third** day that Hapley studied water plants, he (2) **noticed/ignored** a new addition to the local (3) **insect/animal** life. He was (4) **drinking/working** late, and looking down the (5) **bottle/microscope**. With his other eye, he could see the (6) **carpet/table-cloth**. The pattern on the grey cloth was coloured (7) **purple/red**, gold and pale blue. It seemed to start (8) **moving/changing colour**. Hapley (9) **suddenly/slowly** lifted his (10) **arm/head** and looked. Part of the pattern was a (11) **small/large** moth with its wings (12) **closed/spread** out.

CHAPTER 2 (A)

Which of these sentences are true? What is wrong with the false ones?

1   Clayton discovered the ghost at the bottom of the staircase.
2   The ghost had a large, pointed nose and a strong-looking chin.
3   Clayton asked the ghost if he was a member of the Mermaid Club.
4   The ghost looked pleased and said he was a member.
5   He was haunting the club because it was an old building.
6   He told Clayton that he had forgotten how to walk through walls.
7   Clayton was not surprised, and asked the ghost to tell him about it.

CHAPTER 2 (B)

Put the letters of these words in the right order.

Clayton raised his hands again. We were all (1) **snoruve**, and sat watching him. He bowed with (2) **gitydin**, and began to wave his hands and arms. As he came to the end, our (3) **mexecettin** grew. The last (4) **nigs** was to open his arms wide and (5) **dhol** up his face. I stopped (6) **traibghen**. There he stood for one long (7) **tommen**. He was bright and (8) **dilso** in the light of the lamp. From all of us, there was a (9) **higs** of the greatest (10) **fleeri**. It was all (11) **sonsneen**. And then Clayton's face (12) **ghanced**.

CHAPTER 3

Use these words to fill in the gaps: **sigh, statues, picture, wheels, madder, road, park, experience, frozen, traffic, band, heard, grass.**

I have heard or read of no stranger (1) _____ than the one Gibberne and I had that day, after drinking the New Accelerator. We went out into the (2) _____, and carefully studied the (3) _____. The (4) _____ of the bus were moving, although very slowly. The passengers were like (5) _____. We walked towards the (6) _____. There, everything seemed (7) _____ than ever. There was a (8) _____ playing. But all we (9) _____ from it was a kind of quiet (10) _____. People stood on the (11) _____ as if they had suddenly been (12) _____. It was like looking at a great, wonderful (13) _____.

CHAPTER 4 (A)

Correct the ten errors in this description of what Wallace found behind the door in the wall.

Wallace went through the blue door. It closed behind him silently, and he was in the house he would remember all his life. He was filled with joy and sadness. It seemed to be a place where only bad things happened. All its colours were clear and unpleasant. It gave him an enormous feeling of anger, a rare feeling only possible when one is young and sad. Everything was ugly there. Wallace remembered all uncertainties, fears, and worries.

CHAPTER 4 (B)

Put the beginning of each sentence with the right ending.

1 The first time Wallace found the door in the wall,

2 The second time, he was a boy at Saint Athelstan's school,

3 The third time he was going to the station to catch a train

4 The fourth time he was on his way to the House of Commons,

5 The fifth time was as Wallace rushed to his father's house

6 The sixth time, he was walking with Gurker and Ralphs

(a) and could not stop, as the vote was of great importance.

(b) to Oxford, to try to get a place at university, and didn't go in.

(c) in order to say goodbye to him forever, and so he could not go in.

(d) it was October, and he was five years and four months old.

(e) and didn't go in, as he was about to reach the ambition of his life.

(f) and he went past the door in order to get to school on time.

CHAPTER 5

Who said these things? Choose from the following names: **Jennie, Mr Coombes, Mrs Coombes, Mr Clarence.**

1 'Be careful with that piano-stool. It wasn't made for elephants.'

2 'What were you saying about my playing?'

3 'Surely you don't object to a little music on Sundays?'

4 'If you don't care about my reputation, why did you marry me?'

5 'You've changed completely since we were married.'

6 'He hasn't got the slightest sympathy with anything I do.'

7 'If a man marries a woman, he must be prepared to look after her.'

8 'I think a man should have a woman's help, if he isn't mean to her.'

9 'I'm a gentle man until I lose my temper, and then you'll be surprised.'

CHAPTER 6 (A)

The second sentence, (b), in each of the following paragraphs is in the wrong place. Which paragraphs should they go in?

1 (a) The stranger asked Mr Hinchcliff if he was a student.
   (b) It was round and wrapped in silver paper, which he unfolded carefully.
   (c) The stranger stared at Mr Hinchcliff, and then unlocked his bag.

2 (a) The stranger silently took something out of his bag.
   (b) Next he said he was going to give the apple to Mr Hinchcliff.
   (c) He held it out towards Mr Hinchcliff.

3 (a) The stranger said it was the apple of the Tree of Knowledge.
   (b) Mr Hinchcliff said proudly that he was a student of London University.
   (c) Mr Hinchcliff decided that the stranger was mad.

CHAPTER 6 (B)

Put these sentences in the correct order to tell the story of the stranger's apple. The first one is done for you.

1 An Armenian escaped from the Kurds and went up into the mountains.

2 On the third day they came down a slope of rock into a dark valley.

3 As he ran, he fell against a tree and a fruit dropped into his hand.

4 Suddenly the valley was lit from far away, by a golden flame.

5 There was a sound like thunder, and the Armenian turned and ran.

6 At once they realized where they were, and dropped to the ground.

7 Then he climbed up a steep cliff and met a friend who had escaped.

8 Then the Armenian's friend jumped up and ran towards the light.

9 He struggled through a slope covered with tall, sharp-edged grass.

10 They climbed up into the heights and wandered there for three days.

11 It was the fruit of a tree in the Garden of Eden.

CHAPTER 7

Put the letters of these words in the right order.

Mr Fotheringay knew there was something (1) **riyouless** wrong. All (2) **nodrau** him nothing could be seen, in the white (3) **glominhot** and in the dust (4) **wolbn** up by the screaming wind, except (5) **sahep** of earth and (6) **isrun**. There were no (7) **laifraim** shapes. Destruction and disorder lay (8) **veewerhery**. Near him was (9) **stoinghem** that might once have been a (10) **getra** tree. It was smashed to pieces from top to (11) **mobtot**. A little (12) **rhufret** away was a heap of (13) **etons** and twisted metal. Then he (14) **ogrinzeced** it. It was the South (15) **geBrid**.

Oxford
Progressive
English Readers